Literature for Life Series
General Editor : Kenyon Calthrop

Short Stories from Ireland

Selected and introduced by Kenyon Calthrop

Frontispiece by Norma Burgin

Wheaton A Division of Pergamon Press

A. Wheaton & Company Limited, *A Division of Pergamon Press*, Hennock Road, Exeter EX2 8RP

Pergamon Press Ltd, Headington Hill Hall, Oxford OX3 0BW

Pergamon Press Inc., Maxwell House, Fairview Park, Elmsford, New York 10523

Pergamon of Canada Ltd, 75 The East Mall, Toronto, Ontario M8Z 2L9

Pergamon Press (Australia) Pty Ltd, P.O. Box 544, Potts Point, N.S.W. 2011

Pergamon Press GmbH, 6242 Kronberg/Taunus, Pferdstrasse I, Frankfurt-am-Main, Federal Republic of Germany

First published 1979

Printed in Great Britain by A. Wheaton & Co. Ltd, Exeter (BW)

ISBN 0 08 022876 3

Contents

Acknowledgements

For permission to reprint the stories included in this book, we are indebted to:

Jonathan Cape Ltd and Edna O'Brien for "Cords" from *The Love Object*; and to Jonathan Cape Ltd and Liam O'Flaherty for "Going into Exile" from *The Short Stories of Liam O'Flaherty*

Maureen and William Corkery, and Mrs Ellen Plant, for Daniel Corkery's "The Ploughing of Leaca-na-Naomh"

Creative Age Press (a division of Farrar, Straus & Giroux Inc.), Copyright © 1947, for James Reynolds's "The Headless Rider of Castle Sheela" from *Ghosts in Irish Houses*

Victor Gollancz Ltd and Patrick Boyle for "In Adversity Be Ye Steadfast" from *A View from Calvary and Other Stories*

Bryan MacMahon for "The Cat and the Cornfield" from *The Red Petticoat and Other Stories*

Macmillan Publishers Ltd and Walter Macken for "The Conjugator" from *God Made Sunday and Other Stories*

Sean O'Faolain for "Thieves" from *The Talking Trees and Other Stories*

A. D. Peters & Co. Ltd for Frank O'Connor's "First Confession" from *My Oedipus Complex and Other Stories*

William Trevor for "Christmas in London" from *Best Irish Stories 2*

George Weidenfeld & Nicolson Ltd and Edna O'Brien for the extract from *Mother Ireland*

Note: Every effort has been made to trace the copyright holders of the stories reprinted in this collection. We apologise for any inadvertent omission, which can be rectified in a subsequent reprint.

Introduction

The contribution of the Irish writer to writing in English has been immense and nowhere more so than in the field of the short story. The short story is a form which suits the Irish writer, partly because Ireland remains a predominantly rural country in which there are still echoes of the story-*telling* tradition that the rest of us have long since lost. The opening paragraph of, for example, *The Cat and the Cornfield* makes the reader very aware of this.

There are echoes of other qualities too which have been obliterated by our more urban and industrialised way of life: Ireland's Gaelic inheritance and the sense of groping towards the mysteries of the past in *The Ploughing of Leaca-na-Naomh* or the ghost in *The Headless Horseman of Castle Sheela*.

Four of these stories are very much about growing up, and describe experiences which are both common to and yet different from the experiences of those of us who grow up elsewhere. The pervasive influence of the Roman Catholic Church (*First Confession, Thieves, The Pilgrims*) and the possibility of half-understood danger and violence (*The Conjugator*) are obvious differences. The stories of adult life from high comedy (*In Adversity Be Ye Steadfast*) to the lyricism of the very beautiful story of unconsummated love (*Michael and Mary*) show an outlook on life quite unlike anything one would expect to find in England or in English writing. Perhaps, as Edna O'Brien puts it, being Irish is also "a state of mind".

For Ireland is a country which has suffered seven hundred years of political domination and economic subservience. The cruelty and despair caused by the conditions which necessitate *Going into Exile* show this very well.

I have deliberately moved outside Ireland for the last two stories to show how Ireland's often sad history still influences the present. Thus *Cords* shows the conflict not only between generations, but between two very different ways of life. *Christmas in London* shows how England's and Ireland's past history is still with us and the indirect effect of mindless .violence on the innocent of both races.

Some of the writers in this collection are already deservedly world famous, others are not nearly so well known. The Irish short story tradition is so rich and so varied that a collection such as this can only give you a small taste of its richness and variety. I hope that you will enjoy the taste and want to read more.

Kenyon Calthrop

An Extract from
Mother Ireland

Edna O'Brien

But time changes everything including our attitude to a place. There is no such thing as a perpetual hatred no more than there are un-ambiguous states of earthly love. Hour after hour I can think of Ireland, I can imagine without going far wrong what is happening in any one of the little towns by day or by night, can see the tillage and the walled garden, see the spilt porter foam along the counters, I can hear argument and ballads, hear the elevation bell and the prayers for the dead. I can almost tell what any one of my friends might be doing at any hour so steadfast is the rhythm of life there. I open a book, a school book maybe, or a book of superstition, or a book of place names, and I have only to see the names of Ballyhooly or Raheen to be plunged into that world from which I have derived such a richness and an unquenchable grief. The tinkers at Rathkeale will be driving back to their settlement by now I say, and the woman who tells fortunes in her caravan will be sending her child down for the tenth loaf of sliced bread, while a mile or two away in her domain Lady so-and-so will tell the groomsman how yet again she got her horse into a lather, and on some door in a town a little black crêpe scarf dangling from a knocker will have on it a handwritten black-edged card stating at what time the remains will be removed, while the hideous bald bungalows will be mushrooming along the main roadsides. The men will be trying as always to distance their fate either through drink, or dirty stories, and the older women will be filled with the knowledge of how crushing their

1

burdens are, while young girls will be gabbling, to invent diversion for themselves.

It is true that a country encapsulates our childhood and those lanes, byres, fields, flowers, insects, suns, moons and stars are forever reoccurring and tantalising me with a possibility of a golden key which would lead beyond birth to the roots of one's lineage. Irish? In truth I would not want to be anything else. It is a state of mind as well as an actual country. It is being at odds with other nationalities, having a quite different philosophy about pleasure, about punishment, about life, and about death. At least it does not leave one pusillanimous.

Ireland for me is moments of its history, and its geography, a few people who embody its strange quality, the features of a face, a holler, a line from a Synge play, the whiff of night air, but Ireland insubstantial like the goddesses poets dream of, who lead them down into strange circles. I live out of Ireland because something in me warns me that I might stop if I lived there, that I might cease to feel what it has meant to have such a heritage, might grow placid when in fact I want yet again and for indefinable reasons to trace that same route, that trenchant childhood route, in the hope of finding some clue that will, or would, or could, make possible the leap that would restore one to one's original place and state of consciousness, to the radical innocence of the moment just before birth.

The Ploughing of Leaca-na-Naomh

Daniel Corkery

With which shall I begin—man or place? Perhaps I had better first tell of the man; of him the incident left so withered that no sooner had I laid eyes on him than I said: Here is one whose blood at some terrible moment of his life stood still, stood still and never afterwards regained its quiet, old-time ebb and flow. A word or two then about the place—a sculped-out shell in the Kerry mountains, an evil-looking place, green-glaring like a sea when a storm has passed. To connect man and place together, even as they worked one with the other to bring the tragedy about, ought not then to be so difficult.

I had gone into those desolate treeless hills searching after the traces of an old-time Gaelic family that once were lords of them. But in this mountainy glen I forgot my purpose almost as soon as I entered it.

In that round-ended valley—they call such a valley a coom—there was but one farmhouse, and Considine was the name of the householder— Shawn Considine, the man whose features were white with despair; his haggard appearance reminded me of what one so often sees in war-ravaged Munster—a ruined castle wall hanging out above the woods, a grey spectre. He made me welcome, speaking slowly, as if he was not used to such amenities. At once I began to explain my quest. I soon stumbled; I felt that his thoughts were far away. I started again. A daughter of his looked at me—Nora was her name—looked at me with meaning; I could not read her look aright. Haphazardly I went through old family names and recalled old world incidents; but with no more success. He then made to speak; I could catch only broken phrases, repeated again and again. "In the presence of God." "In the Kingdom of God." "All gone for ever." "Let them rest in peace" (I translate from the Irish). Others too there were of which I could make nothing. Suddenly I went silent. His eyes had begun to change. They were not becoming fiery or angry—that would have emboldened me, I would have blown on his anger; a little passion, even an outburst of bitter temper would have troubled me but little if in its sudden revelation I came on some new fact or even a new name in the broken story of that ruined family. But no; not fiery but cold and terror-stricken were his eyes becoming. Fear was rising in them like dank water. I withdrew my gaze, and his daughter ventured on speech:

"If you speak of the cattle, noble person, or of the land, or of the new laws, my father will converse with you; but he is dark about what happened long ago." Her eyes were even more earnest than her tongue—they implored the pity of silence.

So much for the man. A word now about the place where his large but neglected farmhouse stood against a bluff of rock. To enter that evil-looking green-mountained glen was like entering the jaws of some slimy, cold-blooded animal. You felt yourself leaving the sun, you shrunk together, you hunched yourself as if to bear an ugly pressure. In the far-back part of it was what is called in the Irish language a *leaca*—a slope of land, a lift of land, a bracket of land jutting out from the side of a mountain. This leaca, which the daughter explained was called Leaca-na-Naomh—the Leaca of the Saints—was very remarkable. It shone like a gem. It held the sunshine as a field holds its crop of golden wheat. On three sides it was pedestalled by the sheerest rock. On the fourth side it curved up to join the parent mountain-flank. Huge and high it was, yet height and size took some time to estimate, for there were mountains all around it. When you had been looking at it for some time you said aloud: "That leaca is high!" When you had stared for a longer time you said: "That leaca is immensely high—and huge!" Still the most remarkable thing about it was the way it held the sunshine. When all the valley had gone into the gloom of twilight—and this happened in the early afternoon—the leaca was still at midday. When the valley was dark with night and the lamps had been long alight in the farmhouse the leaca had still the red gleam of sunset on it. It hung above the misty valley like a velarium—as they used to call that awning cloth which hung above the emperor's seat in the amphitheatre.

"What is it called, do you say?" I asked again.

"Leaca-na-Naomh," she replied.

"Saints used to live on it?"

"The hermits," she answered, and sighed deeply.

Her trouble told me that that leaca had to do with the fear that was burrowing like a mole in her father's heart. I would test it. Soon afterwards the old man came by, his eyes on the ground, his lips moving.

"That leaca," I said, "what do you call it?"

He looked up with a startled expression. He was very white; he couldn't abide my steady gaze.

"Nora," he cried, raising his voice suddenly and angrily, "*cas isteach iad, cas isteach iad!*" He almost roared at the gentle girl.

"Turn in—what?" I said, roughly, "the cattle are in long ago."

"'Tis right they should," he answered, leaving me.

Yes, this leaca and this man had between them moulded out a tragedy, as between two hands.

Though the sun had gone I still sat staring at it. It was far off, but whatever light remained in the sky had gathered to it. I was wondering at its clear definition among all the vague and misty mountain shapes when a voice quivering with age, high and untuneful, addressed me:

"'Twould be right for you to see it when there's snow on it."

"Ah!"

"'Tis blinding!" The voice had changed so much as his inner vision strengthened that I gazed up quickly at him. He was a very old man, somewhat fairy-like in appearance, but he had the eyes of a boy. These eyes told me he was one who had lived imaginatively. Therefore I almost gripped him lest he should escape; from him would I learn of Leaca-na-Naomh. Shall I speak of him as a vassal of the house, or as a tatter of the family, or as a spall of the rough landscape? He was native to all three. His homespun was patched with patches as large and as straight-cut as those you'd see on a fisherman's sail. He was, clothes and all, the same colour as the aged lichen of the rocks; but his eyes were as fresh as dew.

Gripping him, as I have said, I searched his face, as one searches a poem for a hidden meaning.

"When did it happen, this dreadful thing?" I said.

He was taken off his guard. I could imagine, I could almost feel his mind struggling, summoning up an energy sufficient to express his idea of how as well as when the thing happened. At last he spoke deliberately.

"When the master"—I knew he meant the householder—"was at his best, his swiftest and strongest in health, in riches, in force and spirit." He hammered every word.

"Ah!" I said; and I noticed the night had begun to thicken, fitly I thought, for my mind was already making mad leaps into the darkness of conjecture. He began to speak a more simple language.

"In those days he was without burden or ailment—unless maybe every little biteen of land between the rocks that he had not as yet brought under the plough was a burden. This, that, yonder, all those fine fields that have gone back again into heather and furze, it was he made them. There's sweat in them! But while he bent over them in the little dark days of November, dropping his sweat, he would raise up his eyes and fix them on the leaca. *That* would be worth all of them, and worth more than double all of them if it was brought under the plough."

5

"And why not?" I said.

"Plough the bed of the saints?"

"I had forgotten."

"You are not a Gael of the Gaels maybe?"

"I had forgotten; continue; it grows chilly."

"He had a serving man; he was a fool; they were common in the country then; they had not been as yet herded into asylums. He was a fool; but a true Gael. That he never forgot except once."

"Continue."

"He had also a sire horse. Griosach he called him, he was so strong, so high and princely."

"A plough horse?"

"He had never been harnessed. He was the master's pride and boast. The people gathered on the hillside when he rode him to mass. You looked at the master; you looked at the horse; the horse knew the hillsides were looking at him. He made music with his hoofs, he kept his eyes to himself, he was so proud."

"What of the fool?"

"Have I spoken of the fool?"

"Yes, a true Gael."

" 'Tis true, that word. He was as strong as Griosach. He was what no one else was: he was a match for Griosach. The master petted the horse. The horse petted the master. Both of them knew they went well together. But Griosach the sire horse feared Liam Ruadh the fool; and Liam Ruadh the fool feared Griosach the sire horse. For neither had as yet found out that he was stronger than the other. They would play together like two strong boys, equally matched in strength and daring. They would wrestle and throw each other. Then they would leave off; and begin again when they had recovered their breath."

"Yes," I said, "the master, the horse Griosach, the fool Liam—now, the leaca, the leaca."

"I have brought in the leaca. It will come in again—now! The master was one day standing at a gap for a long time; there was no one near him. Liam Ruadh came near him. 'It is not lucky to be silent as that,' he said. The master raised his head and answered: 'The leaca for wheat.'

"The fool nearly fell down in a sprawling heap. No one had ever heard of anything like that.

" 'No,' he said like a child.

" 'The leaca for wheat,' the master said again, as if there was someone inside him speaking.

"The fool was getting hot and angry. 'The leaca for prayer!' he said.

" 'The leaca for wheat,' said the master, a third time.

"When the fool heard him he gathered himself up and roared—a loud 'O-oh!'; it went around the hills like sudden thunder; in the little breath he had left he said: 'The leaca for prayer!' The master went away from him; who could tell what might have happened?

"The next day the fool was washing a sheep's diseased foot—he had the struggling animal held firm in his arms when the master slipped behind him and whispered in his ear: 'The leaca for wheat.'

"Before the fool could free the animal the master was gone. He was a wild, swift man that day. He laughed. It was that selfsame night he went into the shed where Liam slept and stood a moment looking at the large face of the fool working in his dreams. He watched him like that a minute. Then he flashed the lantern quite close into the fool's eyes so as to dazzle him, and he cried out harshly 'The leaca for wheat', making his voice appear far off, like a trumpet call, and before the fool could understand where he was, or whether he was asleep or awake, the light was gone and the master was gone.

"Day after day the master put the same thought into the fool's ear. And Liam was becoming sullen and dark. Then one night, long after we were all in our sleep, we heard a wild crash.

"The fool had gone to the master's room. He found the door bolted. He put his shoulder to it. The door went in about the room, and the arch above it fell in pieces around the fool's head—all in the still night.

" 'Who's there? What is it?' cried the master, starting up in his bed.

" 'Griosach for the plough!' said the fool.

"No one could think of Griosach being hitched to a plough. The master gave him no answer. He lay down in his bed and covered his face. The fool went back to his straw. Whenever the master now said 'The leaca for wheat' the fool would answer 'Griosach for the plough.'

"The tree turns the wind aside, yet the wind at last twists the tree. Like wind and tree master and fool played against each other, until at last they each of them had spent their force.

" 'I will take Griosach and Niamh and plough the leaca,' said the fool; it was a hard November day.

" 'As you wish,' said the master. Many a storm finished with a little sob of wind. Their voices were now like a little wind.

"The next night a pair of smiths were brought into the coomb all the way from Aunascawl. The day after that the mountains were ringing with their blows as the ploughing gear was overhauled. Without rest or laughter or chatter the work went on, for Liam was at their shoulders, and he hardly gave them time to wipe their sweaty hair. One began to sing ' 'Tis my grief on Monday now', but Liam struck him one blow and stretched him. He returned to his work quiet enough after that. We saw the fool's anger rising. We made way for him; and he was going back and forth the whole day long; in the evening his mouth began to froth and his tongue to blab. We drew away from him; wondering what he was thinking of. The master himself began to grow timid; he hadn't a word in him; but he kept looking up at us from under his brow as if he feared we would turn against him. Sure we wouldn't; wasn't he our master—even what he did?

"When the smiths had mounted their horses that night to return to Aunascawl one of them stooped down to the master's ear and whispered: 'Watch him, he's in a fever.'

" 'Who?'

" 'The fool.' That was a true word.

"Some of us rode down with the smiths to the mouth of the pass, and as we did so, snow began to fall silently and thickly. We were glad; we thought it might put back the dreadful business of the ploughing. When we returned towards the house we were talking. But a boy checked us.

" 'Whisht!' he said.

"We listened. We crept beneath the thatch of the stables. Within we heard the fool talking to the horses. We knew he was putting his arms around their necks. When he came out, he was quiet and happy-looking. We crouched aside to let him pass. Then we told the master.

" 'Go to your beds,' he said, coldly enough.

"We played no cards that night; we sang no songs; we thought it too long until we were in our dark beds. The last thing we thought of was the snow falling, falling, falling on Leaca-na-Naomh and on all the mountains. There was not a stir or a sigh in the house. Everyone feared to hear his own bed creak. And at last we slept.

"What awoke me? I could hear voices whispering. There was fright in them. Before I could distinguish one word from another I felt my neck creeping. I shook myself. I leaped up. I looked out. The light was blinding. The moon was shining on the slope of new snow. There was none falling now; a light thin wind was blowing out of the lovely stars.

"Beneath my window I saw five persons standing in a little group, all clutching one shoulder like people standing in a flooded river. They were very still; they would not move even when they whispered. As I wondered to see them so fearfully clutching one another a voice spoke in my room:

" 'For God's sake, Stephen, get ready and come down.'

" 'Man, what's the matter with ye?''

" 'For God's sake come down.'

" 'Tell me, tell me!'

" 'How can I? Come down!'

"I tried to be calm; I went out and made for that little group, putting my hand against my eyes, the new snow was so blinding.

" 'Where's the master?' I said.

" 'There!' They did not seem to care whether or not I looked at the master.

"He was a little apart; he was clutching a jut of rock as if the land was slipping from his feet. His cowardice made me afraid. I was hard put to control my breath.

" 'What are ye, are ye all staring at?' I said.

" 'Leaca-na—.'—The voice seemed to come from over a mile away, yet it was the man beside me had spoken.

"I looked. The leaca was a dazzling blaze, it was true, but I had often before seen it as bright and wonderful. I was puzzled.

" 'Is it the leaca ye're all staring –' I began; but several of them silently lifted up a hand and pointed towards it. I could have stared at them instead; whether or not it was the white moonlight that was on them, they looked like men half frozen, too chilled to speak. But I looked where those outstretched hands silently bade me. Then I, too, was struck dumb and became one of that icy group, for I saw a little white cloud moving across the leaca, a feathery cloud, and from the heart of it there came every now and then a little flash of fire, a spark. Sometimes, too, the little cloud would grow thin, as if it was scattering away, at which times it was a moving shadow we saw. As I blinked at it I felt my hand groping about to catch something, to catch someone, to make sure of myself; for the appearance of everything, the whiteness, the stillness, and then that moving cloud whiter than anything else, whiter than anything in the world, and so like an angel's wing moving along the leaca, frightened me until I felt like fainting away. To make things worse, straight from the little cloud came down a whisper, a long, thin, clear, silvery cry: 'Griosach! Ho-o-o-oh! Ho-o-o-oh!', a ploughing cry. We did not move; we kept our silence: everyone knew that that cry was going through everyone else as through himself, a lash of coldness. Then I understood why the master was hanging on to a rock; he must have heard the cry before anyone else. It was terrible, made so thin and silvery by the distance; and yet it was a cry of joy—the fool had conquered Griosach!

"I do not know what wild thoughts had begun to come into my head when one man in the group gasped out 'Now!' and then another, and yet another. Their voices were breath, not sound. Then they all said 'Ah!' and I understood the fear that had moved their tongues. I saw the little cloud pause a moment on the edge of the leaca, almost hang over the edge, and then begin to draw back from it. The fool had turned his team on the verge and was now ploughing up against the hill.

" 'O-o-h,' said the master, in the first moment of relief; it was more like a cry of agony. He looked round at us with ghastly eyes; and our eyeballs turned towards his, just as cold and fixed. Again that silvery cry floated down to us 'Griosach! Ho-o-o-oh!' And again the lash of coldness passed through every one of us. The cry began to come more frequently, more triumphantly, for now again the little cloud was ploughing down the slope, and its pace had quickened. It was making once more for that edge beneath which was a sheer fall of hundreds of feet.

"Behind us, suddenly, from the direction of the thatched stables came a loud and high whinny—a call to a mate. It was so unexpected, and we were all so rapt up in what was before our eyes, that it shook us, making us spring from one another. I was the first to recover.

" 'My God,' I said, 'that's Niamh, that's Niamh!'

"The whinny came again; it was Niamh surely.

"'What is he ploughing with, then? What has he with Griosach?'

"A man came running from the stables; he was trying to cry out: he could hardly be heard:

"'Griosach and Lugh! Griosach and Lugh!'

"Lugh was another sire horse; and the two sires would eat each other; they always had ill will for each other. The master was staring at us.

"'Tisn't Lugh?' he said, with a gurgle in his voice.

"No one would answer him. We were thinking if the mare's cry reached the sires their anger would blaze up and no one could hold them; but why should Liam have yoked such a team?

"'Hush! hush!' said a woman's voice.

"We at once heard a new cry; it came down from the leaca:

"'Griosach, back! back!' It was almost inaudible, but we could feel the swiftness and terror in it. 'Back! Back!' came down again. 'Back, Griosach, back!'

"'They're fighting, they're fighting—the sires!' one of our horse-boys yelled out—the first sound above a breath that had come from any of us, for he was fonder of Lugh than of the favourite Griosach, and had forgotten everything else. And we saw that the little cloud was almost at a standstill, yet that it was disturbed; sparks were flying from it; and we heard little clanking sounds, very faint, coming from it. They might mean great leaps and rearings.

"Suddenly we saw the master spring from that rock to which he had been clinging as limp as a leaf in autumn, spring from it with great life and roar up towards the leaca:

"'Liam! Liam! Liam Ruadh!' He turned to us, 'Shout, boys, and break his fever,' he cried, 'Shout, shout!'

"We were glad of that.

"'Liam! Liam! Liam Ruadh!' we roared.

"'My God! My God!' we heard as we finished. It was the master's voice; he then fell down. At once we raised our voices again; it would keep us from seeing or hearing what was happening on the leaca.

"'Liam! Liam! Liam Ruadh!'

"There was wild confusion.

"'Liam! Liam! Liam! Ruadh! Ruadh! Ruadh!' the mountains were singing back to us, making the confusion worse. We were twisted about—one man staring at the ground, one at the rock in front of his face, another at the sky high over the leaca, and one had his hand stretched out like a signpost on a hilltop, I remember him best; none of us were looking at the leaca itself. But we were listening and listening and at last they died, the echoes, and there was a cold silence, cold, cold. Then we heard old Diarmuid's passionless voice begin to pray:

"'*Abhaile ar an sioruidheacht go raibh a anam.*' 'At home in Eternity may his soul!—' We turned round, one by one, without speaking a word, and stared at the leaca. It was bare! The little cloud was still in the air—a white dust, ascending. Along the leaca we saw two thin shadowy lines—they looked as if they had been drawn in very watery ink on its dazzling surface. Of horses, plough, and fool there wasn't a trace. They had gone over the edge while we roared.

"Noble person, as they went over I'm sure Liam Ruadh had one fist at Lugh's bridle, and the other at Griosach's, and that he was swinging high in the air between them. Our roaring didn't break his fever, say that it didn't, noble person? But don't question the master about it. I have told you all!"

"I will leave this place tonight," I said.

"It is late, noble person."

"I will leave it now, bring my my horse."

That is why I made no further inquiries in that valley as to the fate of that old Gaelic family that were once lords of those hills. I gave up the quest. Sometimes a thought comes to me that Liam Ruadh might have been the last of an immemorial line, no scion of which, if God had left him his senses, would have ploughed the Leaca of the Saints, no, not even if it were to save him from begging at fairs and in public houses.

First Confession

Frank O'Connor

All the trouble began when my grandfather died and my grandmother —my father's mother—came to live with us. Relations in the one house are a strain at the best of times, but, to make matters worse, my grandmother was a real old countrywoman and quite unsuited to the life in town. She had a fat, wrinkled old face, and, to Mother's great indignation, went round the house in bare feet—the boots had her crippled, she said. For dinner she had a jug of porter and a pot of potatoes with—sometimes—a bit of salt fish, and she poured out the potatoes on the table and ate them slowly, with great relish, using her fingers by way of a fork.

Now, girls are supposed to be fastidious, but I was the one who suffered most from this. Nora, my sister, just sucked up to the old woman for the penny she got every Friday out of the old-age pension, a thing I could not do. I was too honest, that was my trouble; and when I was playing with Bill Connell, the sergeant-major's son, and saw my grandmother steering up the path with the jug of porter sticking out from beneath her shawl, I was mortified. I made excuses not to let him come into the house, because I could never be sure what she would be up to when we went in.

When Mother was at work and my grandmother made the dinner I wouldn't touch it. Nora once tried to make me, but I hid under the table from her and took the bread-knife with me for protection. Nora let on to be very indignant (she wasn't, of course, but she knew Mother saw through her, so she sided with Gran) and came after me. I lashed out at her with the bread-knife, and after that she left me alone. I stayed there till Mother came in from work and made my dinner, but when Father came in later Nora said in a shocked voice: "Oh, Dadda, do you know what Jackie did at dinner-time?" Then, of course, it all came out; Father gave me a flaking; Mother interfered, and for days after that he didn't speak to me and Mother barely spoke to Nora. And all because of that old woman! God knows, I was heart-scalded.

Then, to crown my misfortunes, I had to make my first confession and communion. It was an old woman called Ryan who prepared us for these. She was about the one age with Gran; she was well-do-to, lived in a big house on Montenotte, wore a black cloak and bonnet, and came every day to school at three o'clock when we should have been going home, and talked to us of hell. She may have mentioned the other place as well, but that could only have been by accident, for hell had the first place in her heart.

She lit a candle, took out a new half-crown, and offered it to the first boy who would hold one finger—only one finger!—in the flame for five minutes by the school clock. Being always very ambitious I was tempted to volunteer, but I thought it might look greedy. Then she asked were we afraid of holding one finger—only one finger!—in a little candle flame for five minutes and not afraid of burning all over in roasting hot furnaces for all eternity. "All eternity! Just think of that! A whole lifetime goes by and it's nothing, not even a drop in the ocean of your sufferings." The woman was really interesting about hell, but my attention was all fixed on the half-crown. At the end of the lesson she put it back in her purse. It was a great disappointment; a religious woman like that, you wouldn't think she'd bother about a thing like a half-crown.

Another day she said she knew a priest who woke one night to find a fellow he didn't recognise leaning over the end of his bed. The priest was a bit frightened—naturally enough—but he asked the fellow what he wanted, and the fellow said in a deep, husky voice that he wanted to go to confession. The priest said it was an awkward time and wouldn't it do in the morning, but the fellow said that last time he went to confession, there was one sin he kept back, being ashamed to mention it, and now it was always on his mind. Then the priest knew it was a bad case, because the fellow was after making a bad confession and committing a mortal sin. He got up to dress, and just then the cock crew in the yard outside, and—lo and behold!— when the priest looked round there was no sign of the fellow, only a smell of burning timber, and when the priest looked at his bed didn't he see the print of two hands burned in it? That was because the fellow had made a bad confession. This story made a shocking impression on me.

But the worst of all was when she showed us how to examine our conscience. Did we take the name of the Lord, our God, in vain? Did we honour our father and our mother? (I asked her did this include grandmothers and she said it did.) Did we love our neighbours as ourselves? Did we covet our neighbour's goods? (I thought of the way I felt about the penny that Nora got every Friday.) I decided that, between one thing and another, I must have broken the whole ten commandments, all on account of that old woman, and so far as I could see, so long as she remained in the house I had no hope of ever doing anything else.

I was scared to death of confession. The day the whole class went I let on to have a toothache, hoping my absence wouldn't be noticed; but at three o'clock, just as I was feeling safe, along comes a chap with a message from Mrs Ryan that I was to go to confession myself on Saturday and be at the chapel for communion with the rest. To make it worse, Mother couldn't come with me and sent Nora instead.

Now, that girl had ways of tormenting me that Mother never knew of. She held my hand as we went down the hill, smiling sadly and saying how sorry she was for me, as if she were bringing me to the hospital for an operation.

"Oh, God help us!" she moaned. "Isn't it a terrible pity you weren't a good boy? Oh, Jackie, my heart bleeds for you! How will you ever think of all your sins? Don't forget you have to tell him about the time you kicked Gran on the shin."

"Lemme go!" I said, trying to drag myself free of her. "I don't want to go to confession at all."

"But sure, you'll have to go to confession, Jackie," she replied in the same regretful tone. "Sure, if you didn't, the parish priest would be up to the house, looking for you. 'Tisn't, God knows, that I'm not sorry for you. Do you remember the time you tried to kill me with the bread-knife under the table? And the language you used to me? I don't know what he'll do with you at all, Jackie. He might have to send you up to the bishop."

I remember thinking bitterly that she didn't know the half of what I had to tell—if I told it. I knew I couldn't tell it, and understood perfectly why the fellow in Mrs Ryan's story made a bad confession; it seemed to me a great shame that people wouldn't stop criticising him. I remember that steep hill down to the church, and the sunlit hillsides beyond the valley of the river, which I saw in the gaps between the houses like Adam's last glimpse of Paradise.

Then, when she had manoeuvred me down the long flight of steps to the chapel yard, Nora suddenly changed her tone. She became the raging malicious devil she really was.

"There you are!" she said with a yelp of triumph, hurling me through the church door. "And I hope he'll give you the penitential psalms, you dirty little caffler."

I knew then I was lost, given up to eternal justice. The door with the coloured-glass panels swung shut behind me, the sunlight went out and gave place to deep shadow, and the wind whistled outside so that the silence within seemed to crackle like ice under my feet. Nora sat in front of me by the confession box. There were a couple of old women ahead of her, and then a miserable-looking poor devil came and wedged me in at the other side, so that I couldn't escape even if I had the courage. He joined his hands and rolled his eyes in the direction of the roof, muttering aspirations in an anguished tone, and I wondered had he a grandmother too. Only a grandmother could account for a fellow behaving in that heart-broken way, but he was better off than I, for he at least could go and confess his sins; while I would make a bad confession and then die in the night and be continually coming back and burning people's furniture.

Nora's turn came, and I heard the sound of something slamming, and then her voice as if butter wouldn't melt in her mouth, and then another slam, and out she came. God, the hypocrisy of women! Her eyes were lowered, her head was bowed, and her hands were joined very low down on her stomach, and she walked up the aisle to the side altar looking like a saint. You never saw such an exhibition of devotion; and I remembered the devilish malice with which she had tormented me all the way from our door, and wondered were all religious people like that, really. It was my turn now. With the fear of damnation in my soul I went in, and the confessional door closed of itself behind me.

It was pitch-dark and I couldn't see priest or anything else. Then I really began to be frightened. In the darkness it was a matter between God and me, and He had all the odds. He knew what my intentions were before I even started; I had no chance. All I had ever been told about confession got mixed up in my mind, and I knelt to one wall and said: "Bless me, Father, for I have sinned; this is my first confession." I waited for a few minutes, but nothing happened, so I tried it on the other wall. Nothing happened there either. He had me spotted all right.

It must have been then that I noticed the shelf at about one height with my head. It was really a place for grown-up people to rest their elbows, but in my distracted state I thought it was probably the place you were supposed to kneel. Of course, it was on the high side and not very deep, but I was always good at climbing and managed to get up all right. Staying up was the trouble. There was room only for my knees, and nothing you could get a grip on but a sort of wooden moulding a bit above it. I held on to the moulding and repeated the words a little louder, and this time something happened all right. A slide was slammed back; a little light entered the box, and a man's voice said: "Who's there?"

"'Tis me, Father," I said for fear he mightn't see me and go away again. I couldn't see him at all. The place the voice came from was under the moulding, about level with my knees, so I took a good grip of the moulding and swung myself down till I saw the astonished face of a young priest looking up at me. He had to put his head on one side to see me, and I had to put mine on one side to see him, so we were more or less talking to one another upside-down. It struck me as a queer way of hearing confessions, but I didn't feel it my place to criticise.

"Bless me, Father, for I have sinned; this is my first confession," I rattled off all in one breath, and swung myself down the least shade more to make it easier for him.

"What are you doing up there?" he shouted in an angry voice, and the strain the politeness was putting on my hold of the moulding, and the shock of being addressed in such an uncivil tone, were too much for me. I lost my grip, tumbled, and hit the door an unmerciful wallop before I found myself flat on my back in the middle of the aisle. The people who had been waiting stood up with their mouths open. The priest opened the door of the middle box and came out, pushing his biretta back from his forehead; he looked something terrible. Then Nora came scampering down the aisle.

"Oh, you dirty little caffler!" she said. "I might have known you'd do it. I might have known you'd disgrace me. I can't leave you out of my sight for one minute."

Before I could even get to my feet to defend myself she bent down and gave me a clip across the ear. This reminded me that I was so stunned I had even forgotten to cry, so that people might think I wasn't hurt at all, when in fact I was probably maimed for life. I gave a roar out of me.

"What's all this about?" the priest hissed, getting angrier than ever and pushing Nora off me. "How dare you hit the child like that, you little vixen?"

"But I can't do my penance with him, Father," Nora cried, cocking an outraged eye up at him.

"Well, go and do it, or I'll give you some more to do," he said, giving me a hand-up. "Was it coming to confession you were, my poor man?" he asked me.

" 'Twas, Father," said I with a sob.

"Oh," he said respectfully, "a big hefty fellow like you must have terrible sins. Is this your first?"

" 'Tis, Father," said I.

"Worse and worse," he said gloomily. "The crimes of a lifetime. I don't know will I get rid of you at all today. You'd better wait now till I'm finished with these old ones. You can see by the looks of them they haven't much to tell."

"I will, Father," I said with something approaching joy.

The relief of it was really enormous. Nora stuck out her tongue at me from behind his back, but I couldn't even be bothered retorting. I knew from the very moment that man opened his mouth that he was intelligent above the ordinary. When I had time to think, I saw how right I was. It only stood to reason that a fellow confessing after seven years would have more to tell than people that went every week. The crimes of a lifetime, exactly as he said. It was only what he expected, and the rest was the cackle of old women and girls with their talk of hell, the bishop, and the penitential psalms. That was all they knew. I started to make my examination of conscience, and barring the one bad business of my grandmother it didn't seem so bad.

The next time, the priest steered me into the confession box himself and left the shutter back the way I could see him get in and sit down at the further side of the grille from me.

"Well, now," he said, "what do they call you?"

"Jackie, Father," said I.

"And what's a-trouble to you, Jackie?"

"Father," I said, feeling I might as well get it over while I had him in good humour, "I had it all arranged to kill my grandmother."

He seemed a bit shaken by that, all right, because he said nothing for quite a while.

"My goodness," he said at last, "that'd be a shocking thing to do. What put that into your head?"

"Father," I said, feeling very sorry for myself, "she's an awful woman."

"Is she?" he asked. "What way is she awful?"

"She takes porter, Father," I said, knowing well from the way Mother talked of it that this was a mortal sin, and hoping it would make the priest take a more favourable view of my case.

"Oh, my!" he said, and I could see he was impressed.

"And snuff, Father," said I.

"That's a bad case, sure enough, Jackie," he said.

"And she goes round in her bare feet, Father," I went on in a rush of self-pity, "and she know I don't like her, and she gives pennies to Nora and none to me, and my da sides with her and flakes me, and one night I was so heart-scalded I made up my mind I'd have to kill her."

"And what would you do with the body?" he asked with great interest.

"I was thinking I could chop that up and carry it away in a barrow I have," I said.

"Begor, Jackie," he said, "do you know you're a terrible child?"

"I know, Father," I said, for I was just thinking the same thing myself. "I tried to kill Nora too with a bread-knife under the table, only I missed her."

"Is that the little girl that was beating you just now?" he asked.

" 'Tis, Father."

"Someone will go for her with a bread-knife one day, and he won't miss her," he said rather cryptically. "You must have great courage. Between ourselves, there's a lot of people I'd like to do the same to but I'd never have the nerve. Hanging is an awful death."

"Is it, Father?" I asked with the deepest interest—I was always very keen on hanging. "Did you ever see a fellow hanged?"

"Dozens of them," he said solemnly. "And they all died roaring."

"Jay!" I said.

"Oh, a horrible death!" he said with great satisfaction. "Lots of the fellows I saw killed their grandmothers too, but they all said 'twas never worth it."

He had me there for a full ten minutes talking, and then walked out the chapel yard with me. I was genuinely sorry to part with him, because he was the most entertaining character I'd ever met in the religious line. Outside, after the shadow of the church, the sunlight was like the roaring of waves on a beach; it dazzled me; and when the frozen silence melted and I heard the screech of trams on the road my heart soared. I knew now I wouldn't die in the night and come back, leaving marks on my mother's furniture. It would be a great worry to her, and the poor soul had enough.

Nora was sitting on the railing, waiting for me, and she put on a very sour puss when she saw the priest with me. She was mad jealous because a priest had never come out of the church with her.

"Well," she asked coldly, after he left me, "what did he give you?"

"Three Hail Marys," I said.

"Three Hail Marys," she repeated incredulously. "You mustn't have told him anything."

"I told him everything," I said confidently.

"About Gran and all?"

"About Gran and all."

(All she wanted was to be able to go home and say I'd made a bad confession.)

"Did you tell him you went for me with the bread-knife?" she asked with a frown.

"I did to be sure."

"And he only gave you three Hail Marys?"

"That's all."

She slowly got down from the railing with a baffled air. Clearly, this was beyond her. As we mounted the steps back to the main road she looked at me suspiciously.

"What are you sucking?" she asked.

"Bull's-eyes."

"Was it the priest gave them to you?"

"'Twas."

"Lord God," she wailed bitterly, "some people have all the luck! 'Tis no advantage to anybody trying to be good. I might just as well be a sinner like you."

Thieves

Sean O'Faolain

From the beginning it was Fanny Wrenne's idea. The whole gang must go up in a bunch to the cathedral for their Easter Communion. This time a real pilgrimage! It would be like walking to Jerusalem. What was more, they must go up there for first mass. Clamorously the gang danced around her.

"Six o'clock mass! We'll have to get up at four. It'll be pitch-dark. There won't be a soul abroad. We'll be all alone. We'll have all Cork to ourselves. Everybody but us snoring." Fanny added her master-stroke. "And after mass, do ye know what we'll do? Buy a bag of broken biscuits and be munching them all the way home."

It was one stroke too many, as they found when they scattered, racing in all directions to beg pennies from their fathers and mothers, their uncles and their aunts, for a bag of broken biscuits.

Were they gone clean out of their little heads? Were they mad? Kids of nine and ten walking half-way across Cork in the dark of an April morning? To a cathedral that was miles away? Supposing it was raining! And what about if they lost their way? Whose idea was this anyway? Fanny Wrenne's. That kid was ever and always creating trouble.

In the end only two of them met at the bridge that morning. Fanny, because she always got her way, because her mother was dead, and her father away at sea, and she an only child, and her old Aunt Kate was a softie. And Dolly Myles, because her father neither knew nor cared what any one of his eleven children did, and because her mother knew that Fanny Wrenne could be relied on to look after anybody anywhere—a dark, sturdy, bosomy, bottomy boss of a robin who would spend her life bullying every other little bird in the garden away from the crumbs that God meant for all. As for poor Dolly, she was born to be bossed. Eyes as blue and as blank as a doll's, her hair as fair, her cheeks as pink, and her adenoidal lips hanging from her nose in such a sweet little triangle that old gentlemen were always stopping her in the street to pat her curly poll.

They approached one another across the bridge like two dwarf ghosts. Upriver all they could see was the bright window of the waterworks shining down on the smooth curve of its lasher. All they could hear was the faint hum of turbines, and even that came and went on the morning wind. Downriver they saw nothing at all but the daffodil of the first gas-lamp, and, far away, one vast cloud reflecting the night glow of the city. Overhead the sky was as black and blue as a mackerel.

Fanny had brought her Aunt Kate's best umbrella. It was red, it bore a red tassel, its handle was a scarlet bird's beak with a glassy eye embedded on each side of its head. She brought it because Dolly had told her the night before that her mother had a good friend named Mrs Levey who lived near the cathedral in a place called Flatfoot Lane. Fanny immediately said they would call on Mrs Levey on the way to mass, and give her the umbrella as an Easter present. In return she would be certain to give them a penny each as an Easter present, and with the two pennies they would buy the broken biscuits on the way home.

The gaslamps were no better than candles. Between their wavering scraps of light they could not so much see the footpath as feel for it with their feet. They walked hand in hand. They did not speak at all. They met nobody. They heard nothing but their own footsteps. Every house was as dark as a prison wall. Then, suddenly in one house they saw a lighted upstairs window. It made them speak. Who could be awake at this hour? Somebody sick? Somebody dying? Staring up at it, Dolly put her arm around Fanny's waist and Fanny clutched the umbrella to her like a baby. Could it be a robber? They hurried on fearfully. Soon they began to dawdle. Once, they looked back towards the west and were glad to see a star floating behind a black cloud. Ahead of them the sky was paling and opening but there was no star to be seen there at all. They sat on a low wall to rest and began to argue about how many broken biscuits you could get for tuppence. They started off again, still arguing, took two wrong turnings and were only half-way up the long sloping street to the cathedral when Shandon Tower exploded into three-quarters chime so close to them that Dolly let out a squeak of fright. *Do. So. La. Re . . . Re. La . . .*

"It's all right," Fanny soothed. "We've lots of time. So long as you know where Ma Levey's house is. And," threateningly, "I hope to God you do!"

Dolly looked down a dark laneway to their right. "I know it's up here somewhere." She looked across the street at the maw of another alley. "Or could it be that way?" Blankly she looked back down the hill. "Or did we come too far?" With a wild rush of assurance she chose the first laneway, and in a second, they were swallowed into its black gullet, running around and around in a whale's belly, through dusky gullies and dark guts, thin defiles and narrow, whirling shafts, dead-end lanes and turn-back cross trenches, all nameless and all smelly, only to find themselves ejected exactly where they began just as a soft sprinkle of April rain began to fall. Seeing that Fanny was about to shout, Dolly got her shout in first. "It must be the other way!" Again they were blown about like two bits of white paper through more revolving lanes, dikes, alley-ways and passages, lined with more dwarfs' houses and whitewashed cabins, some thatched, some slated, each with its holland blind drawn down tightly, all of them so close together that a woman could, without moving her body, have stretched her hand from her own door to her neighbour's for the loan of a sup of milk or to return yesterday's newspaper. In every one of those cobbled lanes there was a runnel, already trickling with rain-water. There was barely room for it between the lines of cabins. There was no room at all for a footpath. They circled and descended, climbed and came down again, twisted and turned until a vast giant suddenly soared up above them with a great black clock face that silently said five minutes to six. At the sight of Shandon Tower where she least expected to meet it, Dolly burst into tears and Fanny, in a rage, pointed the bayonet of her umbrella at her belly.

"The house!" she screamed. "Or I'll spit you up against that wall."

"But," Dolly wailed, "I was only up here once. And I was with me mudder. And it was two years ago. And I was only seven."

"Find that house!"

"If we could only find Flatfoot Lane, I know I'd know the house."

"How would you know it? This place is maggoty with houses."

"It have a white card in the window with Mrs Levey's name on it."

"March!"

Dolly snuffled and pleaded.

"Why can't we keep the umbrella. It's not your umbrella. You stole it. And if it goes on raining we'll be drownded."

At this sign of grace the sky ceased to weep, but the devil smiled. By magic there appeared, just above their heads, a bright red board that said FLATFOOT LANE. Here there were real houses, small but two-storeyed, in red brick, with two windows above and one window and a door below. More cobbles, no pavement, another gurgling refuse runnel and at the end of it a blank wall. They raced up one side of it and down the other, and, at last, there, between looped lace curtains, was the white card. It said in black print MIRIAM LEVEY. Beneath the name it said LOANS. On its green door there was a brassy knocker shaped like an amputated hand. Fanny seized it, sent a rattle of gun-fire echoing up and down the lane, and looked at the upstairs window expectantly. Nobody stirred. She looked across the lane and could just see the tiptop of the clock tower, a tiny green dome carrying a big golden salmon, its weather-vane gleaming in the risen sun and stirring faintly in the morning wind. Still, no sound, not a breath, not a thing stirring except when a white cat flowed along the base of the enclosing wall and leaped over it like a wave.

"Maybe," Dolly said hopefully, "she's dead?"

Fanny sent another dozen rounds of rifle-fire up and down the lane. They heard the upper window squeak open, saw ten bony fingers slide over the windowsill and Mrs Levey's tiny witch's face, yawning up at the sky from underneath a cellophane bag full of white hair in blue curlers. She yawned for so long that they thought she would never close her gummy mouth again. When she had finished her yawning she peered sleepily around the lane, said, "Pusspuss! Pusspuss!" and finally looked down at the two white children. Fanny cheerfully waved the red umbrella at her.

"Good morning, Mrs Levey. Me Aunt Kate sent us up to you with this gorgeous umbrella for a present for Easter."

"Your Aunt who?" she asked, and the word "who" turned into another prolonged yawn. She peered down at the pair of them, shook her head, said, "I'm afraid, child, I don't know no aunts at all. But, anyway, whoever she is. . . ." Another yawn. "Or whatever it is, leave it there on the windowsill and I'll get it when I wake up", and withdrew, and the window banged.

Fanny gazed reproachfully at Dolly, who, knowing what was coming, lifted her blonde eyebrows, put her hand on her hip and, self-dissociatingly, began to examine the architecture of every house along the opposite side of the lane.

"So that," Fanny said scornfully, "is your ma's lovely friend?"

"That," Dolly piped, without as much as a backward glance, "is your aunt's lovely umbrella."

"A mangy ould maggoty ould money-lender."

"Our credit was always good," Dolly said loftily.

Fanny looked imploringly at the sky. The great gong saved her, booming the full hour, and all over the valley lesser bells softly announcing the angelus.

"We'll be late," she shouted, threw the scarlet object on the windowsill and they scurried off back to the open street of the hill.

In the valley spires and chimneys were now tipped by the sun. Between these hill-houses the only sign that the night was going was a man who raced before them, lamplighter by night, lampquencher in the morning, plucking the head off every daffodil as he ran.

They hastened into the cathedral, panting. It blazed with lights, candles and white chrysanthemums. Not more than a couple of dozen worshippers. The priest, robed in the violet of Lent, was standing with his back to the altar, reading from a book the gospel story of the woman caught in adultery. ("What does that mean?" Dolly whispered, and Fanny whispered, "Watering the milk.") Afterwards, Dolly said the bit she liked was where Jesus said to her, "Run along with you, now, but don't do that any more", but Fanny said the bit she liked was where Jesus kept stooping to the ground, writing some strange words whose meaning, the priest said, nobody will understand to the end of time. After that the sermon began and it went on so long that their heads began to nod, and they had to nudge and kick at one another to wake up, then making shocked faces and giggling, or, for fun, pretending to yawn like Ma Levey in the window. At last the priest ended his sermon, throwing his white wings open to say, "Three weeks after He forgave that unfortunate woman they murdered Him, calling Him a criminal, but three weeks from now He will rise again as, in a few minutes, He will appear amongst us in the shape of a white circle, shining and immortal. Leave ye all kneel down now and prepare to welcome Him as He descends from heaven."

The time for communion came. Side by side, their hands joined like the angels in holy pictures, their eyes modestly cast down, they walked slowly to and from the altar rails, as Sister Angelina at school had taught them to do. Slowly, the mass ended. There were more public prayers after it, and then they were standing in the porch, the city below them, the morning about them, the gaslamps all quenched, the pavements dancing with rain. A postman's black cape shone. A milkman, hooped against the wind and rain, raced from his cart to pour milk into a saucer-covered jug on a door-step, leaped back into his chariot and drove off with his whip sailing behind him like a flag.

"What about the umbrella?" Dolly said accusingly, and, because of the rain, longingly.

"Why don't we take it back?" Fanny cried, and hand in hand they galloped down the hill and back into Flatfoot Lane. The trickle of rain-water still ran whispering down the central runnel. In an upstairs window an old man, slowly and dexterously shaving one side of his face before a small square mirror balanced on top of the window sash, suspended his razor to watch them gallop through the rain, halt before the white card and stare at the empty windowsill. Fanny rattled the hand on the green door and peered upward, the rain pouring down her face. The upper window squeaked open and Mrs Levey looked down.

"Oh, Law!" she said mildly. "Is it ye again?"

"We made an awful mistake, Mrs Levey, we brought you the wrong umbrella, would yeh ever throw it down to us and we'll bring yeh the right one tomorrow morning at exactly the same time."

The old face withdrew. After a moment the red object came sailing out through the window over their heads, plonked on the wet cobbles and the window banged shut.

The umbrella was as old as sin. It bulged like a carrot. It was tied by a bit of string. It had a black bamboo handle. The old man in the opposite window, one half of his face red, the other half white, hailed them.

"Use it, girls," he shouted. "That's rain! Oho!" he assured them, waving his frothy razor, "I see it all. Ye gave her yeer lovely new umbrella and she throws ye back her leavings. Just like her!" he roared at the top of his voice across the lane. "The bloody ould Jew", and returned to his tender shaving.

Fanny picked up the carroty umbrella, untied the bit of string, shot the gamp open above her head and from it there showered scores and scores of pieces of paper that the wind at once sent blowing wildly all over the cobbles. The old man, watching, let out a roar of delight that drowned the last strokes of the seventh hour. Others who must also have been watching from behind their curtains, slammed up their windows, leaned out, cheered and bawled and pointed joyfully to one another.

In astonishment the two children stared around them at what they had done. Up and down the lane, more and more doors opened and more people pointed, laughing and shouting in chorus, "Levey the thievey, the dirty ould sheeny, rob ye and leave ye!" Overhead the old woman's window opened. She leaned out, screamed like a peacock, vanished, and the next minute shot past them, a man's overcoat over her head and her night-dress like a shawl, racing hither and thither barefooted over the wet cobbles after her dockets. As she raced and stooped and picked, the whole lane kept bawling their horrid chorus at her. Only once did she pause and that was to shake her skinny fist at them. Then, suddenly, there was total silence. She had collapsed on her hunkers in the middle of the lane, her withered arms raised to the pouring sky, her mouth wide open, pleading to it in some strange language. As suddenly she fell silent, her head and her hands sunk into her lap. Slowly, a handsome young man came forward in his bare feet to lift her. After him an old woman came, and then another, and another, began to pick up the bits of paper, until one by one all the watchers were silently gathering up her dockets and pressing them into her crumpled hands. The two children ran.

Not until they halted at the river did Fanny notice that the rotten scarlet thing had accompanied them. She threw it over the quay wall, where, by stretching up on their toes to look, they could see it floating slowly away on the outgoing tide.

"Down the river!" Fanny hooted.

"Under every bridge," Dolly giggled.

"Out to sea!" Fanny shouted.

Laughing they turned for home, stamping into the puddles of the rain, screaming with delight as they kicked arcs of water at one another. They lifted their wide-open mouths to the trees along the Mall trying to catch the falling drops. When they came to the iron railings opposite their own parish church of Saint Vincent they swung on them like two white wheels to see the rain falling up, and the church spires pointing down, the whole world standing on its head. By the time they came to their own bridge the rain had petered out, the sky was white and blue, the river water was smooth, the fields beyond it were empty and wet.

"Anyway," Fanny said, "even if we got the pennies we couldn't have bought broken biscuits. Not a shop open."

They saw a light in a cottage, and a light in a villa on the side of the hill, and one window in a house beside the river was reflected longingly in the pure water. Dolly cocked her head.

"Listen!" she said.

They listened. Far away, around the bend of the road, from maybe half a mile away they could barely hear it. It would be lighted, and empty. The first tram.

The Conjugator

Walter Macken

My heart nearly stopped beating when I saw him.

It was market-day in the town, and they had set up stalls where men were auctioning off cheap clothes that you could wear-as-you-pay and there were vans selling fish and chips and stalls with jewellery and things like that. It was none of those made me pause but the man standing on the box sending a stream of things rising into the air in front of his face from one hand to the other, plates and coloured balls.

He was a tall man with long hands. I was too far away to hear what he was saying, but I closed on the laughing crowd that surrounded him to get a better look at his face. Maybe, I thought, it is he. I knew it couldn't be but it had always been like this. I always seemed to be searching for him, hoping, and as I moved in now towards this juggler the years seemed to fall away from me; my hair was no longer grey but brown and unruly and needing to be clipped. Sometimes it is easy to shed the weary years.

For I was young when I first met him. I remember we had all enjoyed our first Holy Communion Day a little while back and the loot we had gathered from relations and weeping sentimental women had become exhausted. It must have been summer, too, because we had discarded our shoes and stockings. I can still feel the heat of the pavement under my bare feet.

These pavements were in the poorer part of the town; long streets of houses all joined together, with doors opening on to footpaths and economically lighted with one wooden lamppost in the middle of everything.

There was Jojo and Vincent and Daneen and myself, Tony, and it's funny how you can remember a conversation at a particular time. We were discussing where babies came from. We were doing this seriously so it will show you how much sense we had.

Daneen, who seemed to know more than the rest of us, adopted a horribly superior air, sitting on the pavement, looking knowingly out of the corner of his eye, humming and playing ceaselessly with jackstones. Now and again he would say, "Oh, you poor ignorant children!" until we were becoming sick of him and thinking of attacking him, and we would have, but our eyes were attracted to the fellow at the lamppost.

He had been there some time, but we had paid little attention to him. We found adults boring, and apart from mimicking a street singer, or pelting him with cabbage stalks if he was a poor singer, we never allowed them to interfere with us.

But this fellow was doing something odd. He had about six fist-sized rocks and he was throwing them into the air one after another, juggling with them, sometimes lifting a leg and juggling the rocks with his leg held up. He looked funny. Then he added a good orange to the stones and an apple, and an apple and another orange until he had four fruit and two rocks describing an unceasing circle.

"Look at the gawk," Vincent said.

"Them's real oranges," said Jojo.

"He's not bad," said Daneen.

"Hard apples too," I said.

"We'll go and look at him," said Daneen, rising from the ground. We walked over to him.

He was a tall skinny fellow wearing poor clothes. You could see his feet through his boots. His hair was dark and tangled and he was unshaven, but I noticed that his eyes were very blue and that his teeth were very white. You don't notice things like this about beggarmen generally. Also when you approach them you do so from the windward side because they smell of sleeping-out and unwashed clothes, but strangely enough this one smelt clean, so you could go nearer to him.

We ringed him but he remained unperturbed. His eyes crinkled. Suddenly one after another the fruit flew towards us and we were quick in catching our share.

He leaned against the pole and looked at us. He pointed a finger at us. "Pixie," he said to Jojo; "Whitey" to Vincent; "Pugnose" to Daneen; and "Skinny" to me. We were eating so we didn't mind. But all the same it was apt names he put on the lot of us.

I thought he was unusual, so between bites I asked, "Who are you?"

"I am the Conjugator," he said. "I juggle and I conjure. Watch!" He made movements with his hands and almost as soon as you could say it he had taken a penny from Jojo's nose, a penny from Vincent's head, a penny from the bottom of Daneen's trousers, and lifting my bare foot from the dust there was a penny under it!

We laughed. He was good. You couldn't spot him at it.

Then he juggled with the pennies. "Do you want these pennies?" he asked.

We looked at one another. Pennies weren't so easily acquired in those times.

"Do you want to drown a dog?" asked Daneen.

The Conjugator laughed. "I want information," he said, "I just want to know all the soft touches in the street. A bargain?"

We thought it over. Not for long. We held out our hands and he put the warm pennies in them and we sat on the road around him. We pointed out the soft-touch houses, including our own, which was a betrayal in a way. We just left in one or two old cranks because we wanted a laugh as well.

"Stout men," he said. "If I return to work these streets I will always consult you before my rounds." He mooched at his clothes and a small square package appeared which he pulled at until it opened out into a sort of canvas tray. It contained ribbons and beads and gewgaws, just an excuse for begging. He was cute, you see, bribing us like that beforehand, because I suppose he knew we could make life hell for him while he was on his rounds.

So he winked at us and started.

We sat at the corner watching. He was a charmer. You would see the angry face of the woman disturbed at her work and as he talked you would see the anger melting, her face softening, until finally she would go back into the kitchen for her purse. He was a good worker. He skipped the doors we told him to skip. But all the time he was drawing close to the door of the Great Crank and we were chuckling inside with glee. We encouraged him with nods.

So he knocked at this door and the little dark-faced man appeared. He looked at the pedlar, listened to him, appearing quite amiable, then he retired and came back again waving a big blackthorn stick which he swung straight away.

The Conjugator was nimble, but all the same he got a few great whacks on the back before his running speed outdistanced the reach of the stick. The Crank stood roaring after him, cursing and shouting until he went home and banged the door. Really, it would make anyone laugh.

We weren't afraid of the Conjugator. After all we were four to one, and if we didn't wish it he couldn't be in the street at all, so we sauntered to the corner where he was sheltering.

"Aren't ye great little bastards?" he asked us.

"We forgot him," said Daneen.

"You did like hell," said the Conjugator. "Is that a fair way to act?"

"Let everything calm down and start again," I said.

"Are there many more like him?" he asked.

"No," I said innocently. There were only two more. He sighed and produced four more pennies.

"How many?" he asked.

Glad of his intelligence, we took the pennies and told him the two houses to dodge.

Then we went off and spent the money.

We saw him several times after that. He would seek us out, sit with us, and pretend to conjure pennies from our persons. We got to like him. He didn't talk big, like. He could have been one of ourselves. He took an interest in us, now that he was getting into our houses. He knew our mothers. Yours is the tall one and yours is the dark one and yours is the fair one and yours is the small one. We told him about our families, our brothers and sisters and how unfair our fathers were to us at times. All that.

I forgot to mention that at this time there was a sort of war going on. Arrests and shootings and raids and things, but when you are that young these things don't leave much of an impression on you.

All I remember was the terror that came over me in the middle of the night when the lorries came thundering into the street and we were all dragged out of our beds and had to stand in the kitchen while big frightening fellows with black guns in their hands searched our houses. That's the most I remember, the black guns, and the rest seemed just a nightmare you would have after going to sleep sometimes.

We talked about these things to the Conjugator and Daneen gleefully told about how his brother was up on the roof the last time, how he got out of a window and pulled himself up by the guttering.

The Conjugator praised that and said how clever it was, but unfortunately the next time they came they got Daneen's brother, because they searched the roof. It was the only time I ever saw Daneen crying and the Conjugator patted his back and told him not to worry, that everything would be all right and conjured sweets out of his pocket. They were odd times all right. Jojo's father had a rifle hidden up the chimney and they got that too and gave him a bit of a going over with Jojo's mother watching before they took him away. That was hard on Jojo as you can imagine. But I thought the Conjugator was very kind to him and seemed really sad about it because there were creases between his eyes.

Something odd happened then. My brother Joe was a big fellow. He wasn't skinny like me. He was well filled out. He was in some sort of a job that kept him away from home a lot, selling things or something I supposed, and I remember this incident was the beginning of the end of the whole affair.

It was late evening. The sun was low in the sky and soon we would have to be off the streets. There was a curfew and you couldn't be on the streets without a pass, and you had to have lights out in the house or if you didn't they were liable to send a bullet through the window to remind you.

"The place is getting spun out for me," the Conjugator was saying. "Soon I won't even be able to make the bribe money that I pay you men. Today I only got elevenpence. So my profit is only sevenpence. How am I expected to live on that?"

We were a bit dismayed. "Ah, don't give up for a while," I said. "You can cut the bribe money to a halfpenny a skull until times get better. We'd miss you now if you went."

"Is it me or the money you'd miss?" he asked.

We thought this over. It was a serious question.

"Ah, we like you," I said. "Is that right, fellas?"

They thought it over. Daneen was chewing a bit of stick. He spat it out. "Arrah, don't go away so soon," he said, for them.

They meant this too. I never saw anyone they had taken to like the Conjugator. He rose to his feet.

"Sometimes the nearest and dearest must part," he said. "Look, Skinny, come with me a minute. I want you." He walked me aside. His hand was tensed on my arm. He was hurting me. "I tell you something," he said. "You do what I say, and don't say who."

This was mysterious.

"What's up with you?" I asked.

"I honestly don't know what's up with me," he said. "Listen, tell your brother Joe not to be home tonight. Just that. That's all." He waved to the others and went away, his tattered trousers flapping round his legs.

"What did he want, Skinny?" I was asked. "What was the secret?"

"Ah, nothing, nothing!" I said. "Come on and we'll race round the avenue before curfew." And I set off, having a good start because I thought of it first, but I was worried.

Joe wasn't home. Maybe he wouldn't come home at all, I thought. I was restless. My mother was chiding me. Can't you sit quiet? What's got into you? Why didn't you eat your bread and dripping? I like bread and dripping. I don't know why I couldn't eat it then.

I was in bed when Joe came home. I heard him downstairs, so I ran down in my shirt and I shouted into the dimly lighted kitchen, "Joe! Joe! Go away! Don't stay home! Please don't stay home!" I can still see him, his eyes wide, staring at me.

"Go back to bed, Tony," he said then, pulling on his coat.

My mother was standing there with her hand on her heart, but Joe was on the way out the back door. He could have hardly got out when the butts of guns were banging on the front door and I was up in bed with the blankets pulled over my head and my heart thumping.

So they didn't find him, but you can see how the trouble started. Joe was waiting for me one day when I was coming home from the school. He pulled me into a quiet way by the canal.

"Now, Tony," he said. "Who told you to tell me to go?"

It never entered my head to say anything but what I said.

"Who, the Conjugator," I said. "Wasn't he good? If it wasn't for him they would have caught you."

"Who is the Conjugator, Tony?" he asked me.

I told him about the Conjugator, what a massive juggler he was and a super conjurer.

"When do you expect him back to the street?" he asked. "I'd like to meet him too."

"Oh, that's great, Joe," I said. "You'll love him. He's a nice fellow and he usually comes on the second Saturday."

Then he gave me messages for my mother and we parted.

The Conjugator came back.

I thought he looked sad that day, tell you the truth. He looked around him a lot. He didn't seem at ease. But there were only the four of us in the street, sitting as usual at the lamppost, so he came over to us, and got on his knees and started the business with the pennies. But he wasn't smiling. He had only conjured three pennies when we suddenly noticed the legs of men around us. I didn't know them but they had hard faces. They would frighten you somehow. None of them was Joe. I was wondering why Joe didn't come to meet the Conjugator. One of them said, "Get up!"

I saw the face of the Conjugator going white in front of my eyes as.he rose to his feet. Then he smiled. I saw his long hands fumbling and then they simply spouted pennies all around us in the dust like heavy raindrops.

"I have to go, fellas," he said. "Goodbye. Don't forget to spend the pennies for me."

They walked away one on each side of him and one at his back.

I started up. The pennies didn't seem to matter somehow. I wanted to call out after him, "Hey, thanks for Joe. You were right about Joe!"

But I didn't call. I didn't do anything because I was afraid of these men, dressed like ordinary men, but their faces were tight and I didn't know them.

I thought then, that maybe they were friends of the Conjugator. I walked a little after them.

Before they turned the corner the Conjugator waved his hand at me. That's what I remember so well, the long thin hands and the white teeth in his face. And then he was gone. I felt odd and lonely.

So a few days later when Daneen said, "Did you hear? They shot the Conjugator. It's in the papers. Hey, fellas, did ye hear, they shot the Conjugator!" I wouldn't believe them. Jojo had even seen him, in a street away from ours and he had a cardboard round his neck with the word on it. I couldn't believe it.

31

"But I saw him," said Jojo. "There was a hole in his head. There was! There was! My mother nearly kilt me for looking at him."

We spelt out the bit in the papers about an apparent itinerant and the mystery of his death, but I found it hard to believe. I still find it hard to believe it. I seem to be always looking for him.

That's why I went towards this juggler now, in case it might be he. Because whatever about him, if he died and it was he, he died from a good act. That's what troubles me. He saved my brother Joe. If he said nothing, who would have known about him? If I said nothing about him, who would have known about him? So it was me, in a way, that was responsible. Maybe that's why I am looking for him.

This fellow now wasn't he. He had black greasy hair and bad yellow teeth and there was a smell off his clothes. The Conjugator would never have had a smell off his clothes.

So I walked away from this one. I suppose that is what I will always do when I see a juggler. I will draw close to him in the hope that he will be the Conjugator, even though I know in my heart he never will be.

The Pilgrims

Benedict Kiely

B lue was the colour of the rosary, the colour of the Mother of God, of the hot steam screaming up from the black engine of the sky arched over the morning town and the tiny station. Long before the train started the pilgrims were saying the rosary, a separate rosary in each carriage, blue voices swelling out, falling and rising, to the blue morning. Then with five decades finished the pilgrims rested from praying and talked about the world they lived in, about the town they were leaving and the town they were going to, about the journey before them to the holy place where the brown skull of the martyr dead for centuries was kept as a sign and a memorial in a glass box.

Listening to the talk, he looked out of the window at the coloured advertisements nailed to the railings on the opposite platform. He put his hands on his bare knees, his own flesh touching his own flesh, and shuddered with self-pity at the ignominy of short pants. He thought of the greater ignominy of dry shaves to sandpaper from his cheeks and chin the white cat hairs that were less like a man's beard than they were like the fluff that gathered around what the cat left in the coal-hole. George had long trousers, good grey flannels with a fine crease in them. But then George was a man with seven years' experience of shaving and the brown wisdom of twenty-one in his eyes. George sat facing him and taking a part in the conversation.

The advertisements slowly moved away from him. Wheels clanked, gathering speed, over the metal of a bridge. He looked down at narrow backyards and small windows with blinds still drawn. That was a Protestant part of the town and the Protestants didn't make pilgrimages and stayed in bed on Sunday mornings reading the English newspapers. When his ma and da reached for their rosaries a second time he made a sudden excuse-me noise that could mean only one of two things. He slipped out of the compartment into the empty swaying corridor. He watched the humpy ridges of the roofs going away from him to be swallowed up in the fields. George joined him.

"Your mother sent me out to see were you sick or something."

He said, "I'm not sick or anything."

"They've got praying on the brain in there," George said. "They'll say the fifteen decades of the rosary if the Lord himself doesn't halt them. I can tell by the look in their eyes."

A slow river curved through the green fields.

He said, "Isn't that what a pilgrimage is for? All praying. An excursion is all drinking and fighting."

"And a wee bit of coorting," George said. "But you wouldn't know about that."

"I heard tell of it."

"I was a year in a seminary," George said. "You can't tell me anything about pilgrimages."

"You know everything."

"I know that the people who go on excursions go on pilgrimages too. The only difference is they don't fight and there isn't much drink."

Green was the colour of the fields on both sides of the railway, the colour of childhood and fun and the first kiss.

"Come on up the train," said George. "There might be card-playing somewhere."

From end to end the train was blue with the rosary. They waited in a corner of the corridor outside a lavatory and gave the people time to tire of praying. They slipped into another compartment and sat down side by side. The old lady sitting opposite them manoeuvred her newspaper with the awkwardness of one unaccustomed to reading a newspaper in a moving vehicle. It was a local newspaper with clumsy pages and black blotchy print. She was a small, stout stump of a woman, her long black skirt billowing outwards and downwards to meet the shiny blackness of buttoned boots of patent leather, her solemn black bonnet almost sitting beside her, its ribbons dangling over the edge of the seat like two thin legs. She sighed loudly behind the newspapers. She folded the newspaper into very small folds. It crackled like a fire catching in weeds and dry sticks. Her face was fat with a hard square fatness and two black moles on her forehead were like the tops of screw-nails holding the tough yellow skin in place and preserving it from wrinkles.

She sighed again and said loudly: "It's a terrible thing to read a third cousin's name in the newspaper in connection with something as terrible as a wilful murder."

She was as black as the soot up the chimney, he thought, and her face was as yellow as goose grease. But inside in her mind she was meditating on murder, and red was the colour of blood and murder, and of martyrdom, and the colour of the vestments the priest wore reading the mass in memory of a man or woman who died for the love of Christ.

The other people in the carriage sighed sympathetically. George was curious. George was always curious. Curiosity was stamped all over his thin, freckled face and sharp question mark of nose. It set his round protruding eyes shining like headlights. He leaned across the compartment and tapped the old lady on the knee. She was long gone past the time of life when a stranger's tap on the knee could be interpreted as anything other than courtesy. George said, "Was it that your third cousin murdered somebody, ma'am?"

"He was murdered," she sighed. "Had his poor head battered clean off. On the threshold of his own barn. The motive was robbery."

Her face wrinkled suddenly, the yellow skin defying for a moment the tightening pressure of the moles. It might have been the grimace of great grief or mental agony. It might just as readily have been the satisfied smile of a princess among her courtiers or an actress surrounded by her admirers, of any man or woman becoming for a moment the centre of interest and attention. For everybody in the compartment had suddenly sat up to listen. The case was in all the papers. When she spoke again it was not only to George but to her alert audience, to the whole world of prosaic people who had never a murdered relative.

"God rest the poor man," she said. "He was civil and innocent all the days of his life. Too trusting, by far. Very unlike his half-brother who two years ago had his name in the papers for something similar."

"Was he murdered as well?" said George.

She blessed herself. She said, "God between us and all harm it was worse. Far and away worse. He murdered a poor girl and, by all accounts, marrying instead of murdering would have been better for both of them."

The compartment shuddered.

"They were an unfortunate family," she said. "Those of you that are old enough might remember the time the servant man murdered the three unmarried sisters."

Nobody seemed to remember it. She was queen and mistress of a horrified silence that absorbed everybody except George.

"Colm here heard his grandfather talking about it," lied George.

He indicated Colm by putting his left hand upon Colm's right knee so that Colm for a moment forgot about murder and remembered the mortifying lack of long trousers.

"Well, the grand-uncle of this poor fellow that cut the girl's throat . . ."

"Was he the servant man that killed the three unmarried sisters?"
"No. But he found the bodies. And wasn't the murderer his best friend. They say the shock of the discovery affected the creature's mind. He never did a day's good afterwards. He ended his life by jumping into a canal in England."

George leaned back in his seat and breathed out slowly and audibly. Brown was the colour of freckles and of curiosity and even the brownest curiosity had to come sometime to the point of satiety. Green was the colour of the first kiss given and taken in the quiet corner of a field, and red was the colour of a man murdering a girl that he should have married, and black was the colour of the Devil and of the clothes of a woman who knew too much about murder.

"May God have mercy on all their souls," said George—with a panache of piety.

He raised his round eyes to the white ceiling of the compartment and beyond the ceiling was the blue heaven.

"That they may share in all the grace of the pilgrimage," said the woman.

She whipped out a rosary as long as a measuring-tape and with each individual bead the size of a schoolboy's marble, and before George or Colm could escape, the gentleness of prayer was around them as blue as the air, and red murder was forgotten and martydom and green kisses, and the prayers they said were set like jewels around the mysteries of the resurrection, the ascension, the descent of the Holy Ghost, the assumption, and the crowning of the Mother of God in the blue courts of heaven.

Grey was the colour of age, the colour of the hair of old men and women, of old streets and high tottering houses and ancient towers, the colour of history.

His mother said, "Where were you all the time, boy?"
"Got stuck in the crowd far up the train, Ma."
"Did you say your rosary?"
"We said several," George replied. "Isn't there a great crowd on the pilgrimage?"

Colm's mother smiled and said there was surely. She always smiled when George spoke politely to her and George always spoke politely to elderly ladies who, for some reason surpassing Colm's comprehension, always liked George.

And there most certainly was a great crowd on the pilgrimage. The pilgrims jammed the exits from the platform. The sun was shining. Outside on the roadway a brass band was slowly, solemnly, playing the music of a hymn. Some of the pilgrims began to sing with the band. George and Colm waited cautiously on the edge of the crowd. A thin monkish man coming from behind caught George by the arm. He said, "George. The right man in the right place, the very man I want."

"Hello, Mr Richards," George said. "Hello, Rosaleen."

Rosaleen stood at a little distance and smiled sweetly. Her father was baldheaded and blackavised, as solemn, in his dark suit, as the high grey houses of the antique town, but Rosaleen was plump, pretty, yellow-haired, and her little body curved attractively. George had one eye on the father and one on Rosaleen. Colm had one eye on Rosaleen and one on George. Green was the colour of the first kiss but the colour of the second kiss and afterwards, or the colour of warm curves, could easily be the yellow colour of ripening corn.

"You're an educated young man, George," said Mr Richards.

He handed George a short length of red ribbon.

"Tie this ribbon around your left arm and that'll make you a steward."

George tied the ribbon around his left arm.

"I'm a steward," he said. "What happens now?"

"You stand outside the station and help to direct the people to the church."

"I was never in this town in my life."

"We'll soon mend that," said Mr Richards.

He sketched with a pencil on the back of an envelope. He handed the sketch to George.

"That's the town," he said.

George glanced at the sketch, then put it into his breast pocket with what seemed to Colm a pantomime of carefulness. In the background Rosaleen was laughing silently at the antics of George. The solemn man was looking solemnly at the struggling crowd. He said, "Tell them to go straight down the hill, turn right over the bridge, turn left in the centre of the town and stop at the first church on the right."

George beating time with the index finger of his right hand, repeated the words as if he was memorising them. George was a card. When he had repeated his instructions twice he gave a military salute and said, "Aye, aye, sir." The solemn man didn't even know he was being fooled. Rosaleen was laughing quietly behind her father's back. Yellow and gold were the colours of her laughter and the colours of the strengthening sunshine. Colm wished to God that he could be a card like George.

Headed by the band the pilgrims were going in a shapeless mass down the slope towards the centre of the town. Colm hesitated. He said, "What about directing the people?"

George laughed.

"Would you pay any attention to that holymary of a man? I wouldn't mind directing his wee daughter."

"She's a nice girl."

"She's all that and something else too," George said.

He looked sideways at Colm. He patted Colm's shoulder. He said,

"Take the advice of an older man. Don't worry your head about her or the likes of her. She's bad medicine for the young."

"She's only three years old than I am myself."

George halted to lean on the wall at the side of the road, to look down on the town, streets and houses and factories, on the wide river with two steamers moored at the quayside, and to look across the river at grey steeples that could chime and grey towers that were always silent.

"A girl of sixteen is a lot older than a boy of thirteen," he said. "Especially when the girl is Rosaleen and the boy has short pants."

Colm said nothing. His soul was weak with the bitter shame of those bare knees. The old suit he wore going to school had long pants but his mother wouldn't allow him to wear his old suit on a Sunday and his father wouldn't buy him a new Sunday suit until the one he had was worn out. For a moment, walking in the blinding sun, he understood the colours of anger and murder.

"What I want now," George said, "is something to eat."

They turned to the right over the bridge. The pavements were crowded with pilgrims gulping down the salt air that came blowing in cool from the sea. In the middle of the bridge a girl called to George. She was tall and sunburned and darkheaded and she wore a blue coat. Her voice had all the round, rough, friendly vowels of country places. The blue coat had about it the musky odour of turf smoke and faintly from her clean skin Colm smelled the smell of plain, unscented soap. She said, "George, it's generations since I've seen you."

George eyed her calmly. He said mechanically, "Go straight down the hill, turn right over the bridge, turn left in the centre of the town and stop at the first church on the right."

She wasn't easy to snub. She laughed. She said, "You're as daft as ever, George. You never come to the crossroads now."

"I'm a steward now," he said. "I haven't a minute. I'm run off my feet directing people."

A passing crowd of pilgrims swept between them. Colm saw George moving away speedily across the bridge and he followed as fast as he could, looking back once or twice for a sight of the tall girl. But the crowd had swallowed her and her coat that was the colour of the rosary and the colour of the sea and of the wide river flowing down to the sea. The smell of her washed skin troubled his senses and he marvelled at the greatness of George who could afford to despise such riches.

The big event of the day was the procession and the procession was all the colours of the rainbow: no less than seven bands blaring golden music; the Children of Mary dressed in blue and white; the silken banners of all the confraternities; the Sunday clothes of all the marching men and women; the white surplices of the priests and altar boys; the brown

Franciscans and the white Dominicans, and always the yellow sunlight pouring out of a blue sky and brightening the walls that were grey with age.

Colm liked the procession, the slow solemn movement, the music of the bands, the wind flapping the banners, the watching crowds lining the street that led up to the church where the shrine was. He liked it because, in spite of the indecency of short pants, he walked with the men who walked strongly and steadily and four deep. He was a man moving in a world of men and for a while he forgot the girl with the blue coat and the girl with the yellow hair.

The bands stopped playing as they approached the church. The bandsmen stood in silence at the sides of the street while the procession turned to the right through wide iron gates and went up steps and through a high-arched doorway. Candles burned on a distant altar. Organ music accompanied shuffling steps as the pilgrims filed into the pews. A priest stood waiting in the pulpit, motionless as a statue, until shuffling ceased and the pews were filled. Then he crossed himself with the crucifix of the rosary beads and commenced the rosary. The voices of the pilgrims rose in the responses, swelling upwards and outwards, filling the church up to the carved wooden angels on the high rafters.

Colm and George knelt side by side at the outer end of a pew in the aisle to the right of the pulpit. It was a pleasant enough place to be. The breeze blew cool in through an open doorway. You could look out through the doorway at green trees and sunshine. Colm would have looked out through the doorway all the time but his mother was sitting two seats behind him and he could feel her eyes boring into the small of his back.

The rosary ended. The pilgrims rose from their knees and sat down on the hard seats. The priest said in a loud voice, "The souls of the just are in the hand of God and the torment of death shall not touch them. In the sight of the unwise they seemed to die and their departure was taken for misery; and their going away from us for utter destruction: but they are in peace."

George leaned towards Colm and whispered something unintelligible, then rose from his seat, genuflected, and was gone into the sunshine.

The priest was saying, "As gold in the furnace he hath proved them, and as a victim of a holocaust he hath received them, and in time there shall be respect had to them."

George might be back in a minute. He might have been feeling ill. He might merely have wanted to go out for a mouthful of air. But for some reason that he could not yet quite understand Colm was nervous and fidgety. He listened uneasily to the priest, "The just shall shine, and shall run to and fro like sparks among the reeds. They shall judge nations, and rule over people, and their Lord shall reign for ever."

The space on the seat left by George was cold and empty. He felt it with his left hand. But he didn't risk a sideways look that his mother might consider a yielding to distraction. He kept his eyes on the priest in the pulpit. The priest said, "Words taken, my dearly beloved brethren, from the Book of Wisdom, the third chapter."

Then he led the pilgrims in making the sign of the cross. He cleared his throat, steadied himself by resting the palms of his hands on the edge of the pulpit, and was off into the sermon. He was good for an hour at least, thought Colm, looking at the size of him and listening to the sound of him, and George was gone like a spark among the reeds, but not in the least like one of the just. For the just who had in the sight of the unwise seemed to die had hardly bothered much about maidens with yellow hair, and Colm's instinct, shivering on the threshold of knowledge, told him that Rosaleen was gone also, like a yellow flame between grey, ancient walls. He rested his hands on his bare knees and gritted his teeth. George had known that he couldn't follow because his mother's eyes were nailing him to his place on the hard wooden seat. That thought set a red mist before his eyes and the priest and the pulpit and the pilgrims faded away and the words of the sermon thundered in his ears as if God were speaking to him alone.

Afterwards, searching the town for George, the words came back to him and fragments of the ceremony that followed the sermon.

He leaned on the parapet of the bridge, losing his own identity in the movement of the blue water going in one mass and glittering with the sun to the neighbouring sea.

After the text the preacher had said, "These words apply most appropriately, dear brethren, to the martyr whose memory we celebrate today."

So many centuries had turned the town grey, all the time the river flowing down to the sea, since the martyr had lived the life of a wandering hunted man. The preacher had preached about those wanderings, about the journey to Europe and the quiet years spent there in studious and cloistered preparation, about the return to Ireland in a small ship sailing precariously over stormy seas. The preacher had gone into great detail about the perils of stormy seas. Studying the smooth movement of the river, Colm tried to imagine what a stormy sea looked like: dark water rising and falling under dark skies.

The preacher had gone into greater detail about the wandering years that followed the martyr's return to Ireland: the minister of a proscribed religion going from house to house with a price on his head, celebrating mass in open places when the hills were white with snow. White was the colour of silence and of eternity. The preacher had grown red in the face and loud with anger when he came to the capture, the betrayal by false friends, the lying charges, the torture and brutal execution.

With his left hand Colm felt the cold empty seat where George had sat: the false friend gone with a girl whose hair was yellow like gold, the yellow gold of the lifted monstrance, the gold of the flames of the candles burning on the altar, the golden voices of the choristers singing Latin words in praise of God, chanting Latin words as the pilgrims filed one by one past the shame of the martyr and out again into golden sunshine.

Once in the course of his search for George he saw his father and mother at a distance along a crowded street. He was hungry and he guessed they were on their way to have tea before the train left. But he stifled his hunger and avoided them, running along a side street that narrowed to a lane and along the lane until it changed into a path that went by the side of the river and away from the town. He followed the path, the gossiping water to his right and a whispering meadow to his left, until the town was far behind him, and the sunlight weakening, and shadows gathering in corners of distant fields.

He found George and Rosaleen sitting on the grass by the edge of the path. George had his legs crossed like a tailor squatting. He was chewing a piece of grass and saying something to Rosaleen out of the corner of his mouth. Rosaleen was combing her yellow hair, her arms raised, her soft mouth fenced with hairpins, her breasts and shoulders disturbed with laughter at the humour of what George was saying.

"Fancy meeting you here," George said.

"It's a free country, isn't it?"

"It's all that and heaven too," George said.

He stood up and stretched himself lazily.

"Is the praying all over?"

"It is."

"My apologies for deserting you," George said. "But I couldn't wait to hear about the martyr's sufferings. It would have broken my heart."

Rosaleen, standing straight while George dusted fragments of grass from the back of her skirt, tinkled with merriment. George grinned. Colm smiled weakly. Slowly and silently they walked back towards the town, Rosaleen walking between George and, Colm, Rosaleen and George holding hands and now and again pressing against each other. The river went gossiping beside them and the whispering of the meadow grass died away into shadows.

In the crowded street near the big bridge they came so suddenly on his father and mother that he had no time to run or dodge. His mother said, "Where were you all the time, boy? We searched the town for you."

"We went walking after the devotions," George said. "Wasn't it a fine sermon?"

A lie no matter how shameless, was never the least trouble to lucky George.

"It was indeed," his mother said. "But you'd want to hurry to get something to eat before the train goes."

"I'm waiting for the late train," George said.

"Can't I wait too?" he asked.

"Indeed you can't," his mother said. "It's all very well for George. George is a grown man."

She looked at George and George looked at her and they laughed with understanding.

Walking away between his father and mother he didn't speak a word, didn't look back once over his shoulder. He knew that George and Rosaleen were going somewhere hand in hand and that they had already forgotten about him.

There was no room for him in the compartment so his mother sent him up the train to find a seat for himself. From end to end the train was blue-black with the rosary. He stumbled along the swaying corridor looking into compartment after compartment, seeing quiet hands holding rosary beads and quiet faces with eyes staring into infinity. Nobody noticed him, a pale face passing the glass, a small boy staggering along the corridor, weak and shivering and ready to cry with the overpowering force of his anger. The train was crowded. There was no room for him in any compartment.

He went on until a doorknob refused to turn in his hand and he knew that there was nothing but the engine, steel and coal as black as night and the Devil. Holding the doorknob in his two hands he sobbed painful dry sobs. What had the martyr suffered that was worse than this: the shame and ignominy and humiliation, the bullying and the betrayal. He turned back down the corridor, looking mechanically into compartment after compartment, looking suddenly into one pair of eyes that did not stare into infinity. It was the girl with the blue coat and the sight of her renewing his agony he fled, hiding for a while in a dimly lighted water-closet, watching his pale reflection in a dirty, spotted mirror. When he opened the door and came out into the corridor she was standing patiently waiting.

"Hello," she said. "You left George behind you."

"George left me."

The light in the corridor was blue, a lighter shade than the blue of her coat. The rocking of the train bumped them suddenly against each other, he steadied himself, his right hand on her shoulder.

"That's a way George has," she said bitterly. "Leaving people behind him."

Looking over her shoulder into the darkness he knew how she had been hurt when George snubbed her, hurt painfully somewhere behind her loud talk and careless laughter.

"A person like George always meets his match," she said. "He won't leave the girl with the yellow hair."

They stood side by side in the corridor looking out into the black world that was spotted now and again with the light in the window of some farmhouse. Their shoulders touched. He pressed closer. His nose was once

42

again troubled with the odour of skin scrubbed clean with plain, unperfumed soap. Her left arm was around his shoulders, the way two friendly boys might walk home from school.

"Do you ride a bike?" she asked.

"I do."

"Then you should cycle out to the crossroads."

"What for?"

"We have great fun there in the evening. Dancing to the bagpipes and everything."

He didn't like dancing. He didn't like the bagpipes, but he knew that dancing and the bagpipes could be the beginning of something. Sitting in loneliness and anger could only be the end of everything: sitting in loneliness and anger remembering George and yellow-haired Rosaleen walking hand in hand beside the smooth river and the lovely shadowy evening going behind them and gathering in the old streets and around the towers and spires. Remembering was death. Cycling and dancing to bagpipes and smelling the smell of plain soap was life.

"I'll go out surely," he said.

Her arm tightened about his shoulders. He turned towards her and kissed her. He had to raise himself a little on tiptoes in order to reach her lips. She had to steer her own mouth carefully down to his. He had never kissed a girl before and, anyway the train was jolting wildly from side to side. He smelled and tasted the cigarettes she had been smoking.

From end to end the train was blue-black with the rosary. Blue was the colour of the rosary, the colour of the Mother of God, of the light in the corridor and the coat that covered the body of the laughing, sunburned girl. Black was the colour of the night all around them, of mouth finding mouth in the darkness making a beginning and an end.

The Cat and the Cornfield

Bryan MacMahon

In Ireland, all you need to make a story is two men with completed characters—say, a parish priest and his sexton. There at once you have conflict. When, as a foil for the sexton, you throw in a mature tinker girl, wild and lissom, love interest is added to conflict. And when, finally, you supply a snow-white cat, a cornfield, and a shrewish woman who asks three questions, the parts if properly put together should at least provide a moderate tale.

The scene is laid in a village asleep on a summer hill: the hour of the day is mid-morning. The village is made up of a church that lacks a steeple, a pair of pubs—one thatched and the other slated—with maybe a dozen higgledy-piggledy houses divided equally as between thatch and slate. The gaps between the houses yield glimpses of well-foliaged trees beyond which the countryside falls away into loamy fields.

On the morning of our story, the sexton, a small grumpy fellow of middle age with irregular red features, by name Denny Furey, had just finished sweeping out the brown flagstones of the church porch. He then took up the wire mat at the door and tried irritably but vainly to shake three pebbles out of it.

At the sound of the rattling pebbles, the sexton's white cat which was sitting on the sunny wall of the church beside his master's cabin, looked up and mewed soundlessly.

Denny glanced sourly at the cat. "Pangur Bán," he said, "if you didn't sleep in my breeches and so have 'em warm before my shanks on frosty mornings, I'd have you drowned long 'go!" The cat—he had pale green eyes and a blotch on his nose—silently mewed his misunderstanding.

Suddenly there came a sound of harness bells. A tinker's spring-cart, painted bright green and blue, with a shaggy piebald cob between the shafts, drew slowly past the church gate. Sitting on the near wing of the cart was a tinker girl wearing a tartan dress and a bright shoulder-shawl. Eighteen, perhaps; more likely, nineteen. She had wild fair hair and a nut-brown complexion. Spying the sexton struggling with the mat, her eyes gleamed with puckish pleasure.

Meeting her gaze, Denny grimaced ill-temperedly and then half-turned his back on her. As on a thought, he swung around to scowl her a reminder of her duty. Slowly the girl cut the sign of the cross on herself.

Just beyond the church gateway, the cob's lazy motion came to a halt. The girl continued to stare at the sexton. Angrily Denny dropped the mat. Swiftly he raised his right hand as if he had been taken with a desire to shout "Shoo! Be off with yourself at once!" The words refused to come.

Pangur Bán raised himself on shuddering legs, arched his back and sent a gracious but soundless mew of welcome in the girl's direction.

"That you may be lucky, master!" the tinker girl said. Then: "Your wife—have she e'er an old pair of shoes?"

"Wife! Wife! I've no wife!" Denny turned sharply away and snatched up his brush.

The girl watched as the sexton's movements of sweeping became indefinably jaunty. Then her smiling eyes roved and rested for a moment on the thatched cabin at the left of the church gate.

Without turning round, Denny shouted, "Nothing for you today!"

The girl was slow in replying. Her eyes still fast on the cabin, she said, "I know you've nothin' for me, master!" She did not draw upon the reins.

Denny stopped brushing. His stance indicated that again he was struggling to say "Be off!" Instead of speaking, he set his brush against the church wall, turned his head without moving his shoulders, and looked fully at the girl. She answered his eyes with frankness. They kept looking at one another for a long time. At last, his altering gaze still locked in hers, Denny turned his body around.

As if caught in drowse, Denny set aside his brush. He donned his hat, then walked slowly towards the church gate. Lost rosaries clinked as the white-painted iron yielded to his fingers. Denny looked to left and to right. Up to this their eyes had been bound fast to one another.

The sunlit village was asleep. Pangur Bán lay curled and still on the warm wall.

A strange tenderness glossed Denny's voice. "Where are you headin' for?" he asked. The gate latched shut behind him.

"Wherever the cob carries me!"

Again the girl's gaze swivelled to the cabin. "Is that your house?" she asked, and then, as she glanced again at the wall: "Is that your cat?"

"Ay. . . . Ay!"

For a long while the girl kept looking at the little house with its small deeply recessed windows. She noted well the dark-green half-door above which shone a latch of polished brass.

"Do you never tire of the road?" Denny asked.

"Do you never tire of being fettered?" the girl flashed. She had turned to look at him directly.

Both sighed fully and deeply. Under the black hat Denny's eyes had begun to smoulder.

Secretly the girl dragged on the rein. As the cob shifted from one leg to another, she uttered a small exclamation of annoyance. Her red and green skirt made a wheel as she leaped from the vehicle and advanced to make an obscure adjustment to the harness. This done she prepared to lead her animal away.

Denny glanced desperately around. Uproad stood a hissing gander with his flock of geese serried behind him.

"I'll convey you apass the gander!" he blurted.

The tinker girl glanced at the gander; her mouth corners twitched in a smile. She made a great to-do about gathering up the reins and adjusting her shawl. As she led the animal away, Denny moved to the far side of the road and kept pace with her as she went. Walking thus, apart yet together, they left the village and stepped downhill. Once the sexton glanced fearfully over his shoulder; the village was not so much asleep as stone dead.

As the white road twisted, the village on the hillock was unseen. The cob—a hairy, bony animal—moved swiftly on the declivity so that Denny had to hurry to keep up with the girl and her animal.

The splendour of the summer accompanied them. The gauds of the harness were winking in the bright light. The countryside was a silver shield inclining to gold. Their footfalls were muted in the limestone road dust. Muted also were the noise of the horse's unshod hoofs and the ringing of the harness bells. At last they came to the foot of the hillock. Here the road ran between level fields. Denny looked over his shoulder and saw Pangur Bán fifty yards behind him walking stealthily on the road margin.

"Be off!" the sexton shouted.

Pangur Bán paused to utter his soundless mew.

The girl smiled. They walked on for a space. Again Denny turned. "Be off, you Judas!" he shouted. He snatched up a stone and flung it at the cat.

The instant the stone left the sexton's hand, Pangur judged that it was going to miss him. He remained utterly without movement. When the stone had gone singing away into stillness, the cat went over and smelled at a piece of road metal the bounding stone had disturbed. Pangur mewed his mystification into the sky; then spurted faithfully on.

The road again twisted. Now it was commanded by the entrance to the village on the hillock.

Here in a cornfield at the left-hand side of the road, the ripening corn was on the swing from green to gold. The field was a house of brightness open to the southern sky. Directly beside their boots a gap offered descent to the sown ground. The cob stopped dead and began to crop the roadside grass.

"Let us sit in the sun," the sexton ventured. He indicated the remote corner of the cornfield.

The girl smiled in dreamy agreement. With slow movements she tied her cob to the butt of a whitethorn bush. The pair walked along by the edge of the corn and sat down on the grassy edge of the farthest headland. Here the corn screened them from the view of a person passing on the road. The fierceness and lushness of growth in this sun-trap had made the hedge behind them impenetrable. Denny set his hat back on his poll. Then he took the girl's hand in his and began to fondle it. Points of sweat appeared on his agitated face.

Twice already, from the top of the grassy fence, Pangur Bán had stretched out a paw in an attempt to descend into the cornfield. On each occasion thistles and thorns tipping his pads had dissuaded him from leaping. Through slim up-ended ovals of dark pupil the cat ruefully eyed the cropping horse, then turned to mew his upbraiding in the direction of his master. Tiring of this, he settled himself patiently to wait.

Pangur Bán sat with his tail curled around his front paws. His eyes were reluctant to open in the sunlight. His ears began to sift the natural sounds of the day.

Reading his Office, the huge old priest walked the village. Glancing up from his breviary, he noticed the brush idle against the church wall: he also spied the wire mat that lay almost concealed on the lawn grass. The impudence of the gander the priest punished with a wave of his black-thorn stick. Standing on the road in front of the sexton's cabin, he sang out, "Denny! Denny Furey!" There was no reply.

The priest shuffled to the church door and in a lowered voice again called for his sexton. At last, with an angry shrug of his shoulders, he again turned his attention to his breviary. Still reading, he sauntered down-hill and out into the open country.

After a while he raised his eyes. First he saw the black and white pony, then he spied the flame that was the cat burning white beside the olive cornfield.

The old man's face crinkled. He grunted. Imprisoning his stick in his left armpit, he began to slouch in the direction of Pangur Bán. From time to time his eyes strayed over the gilt edging and the coloured markers of his book.

Denny glanced up from his sober love-making.

"Divine God!" he exclaimed.

The girl was leaning back on the grass: her doing so had tautened a swath of green hay to silver. She was smiling up at the sky as she spaced her clean teeth along a grass stem.

Reaching the cat, the priest halted. "Pangur Bán," he wheedled in a low voice. His eyes were roving over the cornfield. The cat tilted his back against the lower may leaves, set his four paws together and drooped as if for a bout of languid gaiety.

For a moment or two the priest tricked with the cat. Then he threw back his shoulders. "To think that I don't see you, Denny Furey!" he clarioned.

Denny and the girl were silent and without movement. About them the minute living world asserted itself in the snip of grasshoppers.

Again the priest thundered, "Nice example for a sexton!"

The sweat beaded above Denny's eyebrows. His legs began to shiver in the breeches his white cat slept in. The girl peered at the priest through the altering lattice of the cornheads. Her expression was quizzical as she glanced at Denny.

From the roadway came again the dreaded voice: "If it's the last thing I do, Denny Furey, I'll strip you of your black coat!"

At this moment a shrewish woman, wearing a black and green shawl, thrust around the bend of the road. She was resolutely headed for the village.

Seeing the woman approach, the priest quickly turned his face away from the cornfield and resumed his pacing along the road. His lips grew busy with the Latin psalms. Peeping out and recognising the newcomer, Denny Furey at first swore softly, then he began to moan. "The parish will be ringin' with the news before dark!" he sniffled.

The woman blessed the priest so as to break him from his Office: then in a tone of voice that expressed thin concern: "Did I hear your voice raised, Father?"

The priest lowered his shaggy eyebrows. "Sermons don't sprout on bushes, my good woman!"

"Ah! Practisin' you were!"

Her crafty eyes alighted on the white cat. "Would it be bird-chasin' the sexton's cat is?"

"It could be, now that you mention it!"

There was a pause. The conversation of the wheat spars was only one step above silence. Flicking the cornfield and the cart with a single glance, the woman said, in a half-whisper, "People say that tinker girls 'd pick the eye out of your head!"

"Did you never hear tell of the virtue of charity, woman?" the priest growled.

The woman made her grumbled excuses. It suited the priest not to accept them. Hurriedly she walked away. Resentment was implicit in the puffs of road dust that spouted from beneath her toe-caps. Before the village swallowed her up, she looked over her shoulder. The priest was standing in mid-road waiting to parry this backward glance.

Again the priest turned his attention to the cornfield. With a sound half-grunt, half-chuckle, he untied the cob, and leading it by the head, turned away in the direction of the village.

The instant the harness bells began to ring, the tinker girl sprang to her feet and raced wildly but surefootedly along the edge of the cornfield. "Father!" she cried out. "Father!"

The priest came to a halt. Well out of the range of his stick, the girl stopped. "So I've drawn you, my vixen!" the priest said.

Breathlessly, the girl bobbed a half-curtsy.

"What're you goin' to do with my animal, Father?"

"Impounding him I am—unless you get that sexton o' mine out of the cornfield at once."

The girl leaped on to the low fence. "Come out o' the cornfield," she shouted. "I want to recover my cob!"

There was a pause. Then Denny shuffled to his feet. The cat stood up and mewed loyal greetings to his lord.

The priest stood at the horse's head. The angry girl was on the fence: her arms akimbo. Shambling dismally, Denny drew nearer. When he had reached the roadway, the tinker girl cried out, "I was goin' my road, Father, when he coaxed me into the cornfield!"

Denny opened his mouth, but no words came. He began to blink his moist eyes. His mouth closed fast. He kept his distance from the priest's stick. As Pangur Bán began rubbing himself against the end of the beloved breeches, the sexton gave the cat the side of his long boot and sent him careering into the bushes.

"*A chait*, ou'r that!" he said.

"Aha, you scoundrel!" the priest reproved. "Can you do no better than abuse a dumb animal?"

Turning to the girl: "Take your cob! And if I catch you in this village again, by the Holy Man, I'll give you the length and breadth of my black-thorn!"

"He said he'd convey me apass the gander, Father!"

Three times she lunged forward. Three times her buttocks winced away. At last she mustered courage enough to grasp the winkers. Clutching the ring of the mouthpiece, she swung the pony downroad. When she had gained a few yards she leaped lightly on to the broad board on the side of the cart and slashed at the cob's rump with the free dangle of the reins. The animal leaped forward.

The priest, the sexton, the cat. The sunlit, rustling cornfield.

"Come on, me bucko!" the priest said grimly.

He began to lead the way home. The sexton trailed a miserable yard or two behind. Glory was gone out of his life. The wonderful day seemed to mock him. The future was a known road stretching before his leaden legs. What he had thought would prove a pleasant bauble had turned to a crown of thorns. In the past, whenever he had chafed against the drab nature of his existence, he had consoled himself thus: "One day, perhaps today, I'll run and buy me a hoop of bright colours."

Denny began to compare his soul to a pebble trapped in a wire mat of despair.

Gradually the priest became infected with Denny's moroseness. Side by side, the priest and his sexton continued to move homewards. In the faraway, the sound of the harness bells was a recessional song of adventure.

Behind the pair and at a discreet distance, Pangur Bán travelled quietly. Now and again he paused to mew his loyalty into the sunny world.

The Headless Rider of Castle Sheela

James Reynolds

Colour is a magic quality in this world. Colour takes many forms. There is the colour spectrum. There is the aura of colour surrounding a given person or place. The name of a family is often synonymous with colourful and exciting happenings in a house or locality. This is very true in the case of the "Marvellous Mallorys" of Castle Sheela. The family of Mallory, once Mael-ora, is large. Its ramifications are formidable and far flung. The term "marvellous" is in effect a title. It might almost have been conferred by some monarch of a realm. Instead it is bestowed by all sorts of people, mostly with awe, now and again with jealousy, even with hate, as this story will bear out.

The village of Galtymore is near the demesne gates of Castle Sheela. The post intended for the Mallorys is sorted and dropped into "the Castle bag" by old Mrs Carmody, the postmistress. It is she who best applies the word "marvellous" to the Mallorys. One day, holding at arm's length a rose-coloured, crested envelope, covered with foreign stamps, postmarks, and forwarding addresses, the captivated Mrs Carmody said, "Great marvels happen in the lives of all those Mallorys. Half the time they're walkin' the world, and the rest of the time they receive letters from it."

Hitching her square-cut spectacles a shade higher, she continued, "They get letters from kings and potentates. In me mother's day, old Lady Mallory'd a letter from the Pope in Rome!"

Mrs Carmody seems to have capped the issue squarely. Marvels follow some people, to colour their lives, as ill luck trails the less fortunate.

To Mrs Carmody I am enormously indebted in more ways than I can name. During my gathering of notes for this story, she answered a thousand questions, answered them with authority and great good humour, a wide smile or a tch-tch-tch, as she thought proper to the mood.

Her wit is expansive, crisp, and boundless. Colour and graciousness enfold this Irish countrywoman, the like of a richly embroidered cloak.

With the early Mallorys we are not concerned in this narrative. The family flourished early on, in Irish history, and stems from antiquity. As an old man of the roads once told me when I asked him where a certain family had come from, "Arragh, yer honour, nobody rightly knows the time. They rose out of a pile of stones, back and beyond in Fermanagh." The first Gaelic castle was a low, square pile of stones. The County Fermanagh is the antique cradle of many Gaelic families. With the exception of Turlough Mael-ora, who fought the Danes at the Battle of Clontarf in 1100, there is no early hero. The Mallorys have shone mostly under two crowns, which they adjusted on their handsome heads at will—sports and society.

In 1722, Brendan Mallory built a huge square house in the shadow of a half-ruined tower which had been built originally by Turlough Mael-ora to quarter his men and horses during the Battle of Clontarf. Later it was made habitable, and various members of the family lived there. One was an abbot; Brother Constantine he called himself. This Mallory abbot was a man of great piety, and it is said he founded an order of monks who lived in the tower for years. After he died and the present Castle Sheela was built, his forbidding presence was still felt. The gaunt, ivy-hung tower points a finger skyward and a shadow across the façade of Castle Sheela, as if to remind the gay, heedless, riotously living Mallorys that frivolity has no lasting substance, is but a pitfall for the soul. It is as if the old abbot continuously reminds his relatives that a seat in the Kingdom of Heaven awaits them, but only by the skin of their teeth will they make it.

In the vicinity of Galtymore—indeed, as far afield as Waterford, Cork and Dublin—if one so much as mentions the name of Mallory, some listener is bound to look up and ask sharply, "The Mallorys? Which one? What have they done now?"

The family reached its peak of brilliant showmanship during the century between 1740 and 1850. During that period two of the male Mallorys contracted marriages with European women. These alliances brought Latin and Tartar-Hungarian blood into the family, thereby adding a veritable rainbow of colour to the already dazzling colour chart of the Irish Mallorys.

In 1739, Galty Mallory, the eldest son and heir to Castle Sheela, made the Grand Tour on the Continent. At that time Budapest was, to most European travellers, like a city on another planet. Travel over tortuous, brigand-infested mountain passes was a thing only the most daring and hardy man would attempt. The heavy spring and autumn rains in that part of the continent made long coach journeys unthinkable for three-fourths of the year. Budapest, therefore, sat in red, gold, and white barbaric splendour on the banks of the swiftly flowing Danube, brushing herself free from Turkish occupation, which she had endured for many years, without losing a sliver of her unique quality. Spread out behind Budapest, the like of a fabulously long train, billowed the Puszta, a vast, mirage-haunted plain.

Galty Mallory decided he wanted to visit this storied city of the Magyars. No roads of this world held any fears for Galty, so one spring day he set out from Vienna for Budapest, travelling by coach and later on horseback. For a part of the way the mud was nearly impassable. Then, as he came out of the Carpathian passes, down into the flat stretches of the Hungarian plain, oceans of spring greenness assailed him. He crossed the Puszta through acres and acres of wild flowers and waving spring wheat. Sitting astride his tired horse outside Budapest, Galty knew instantly that all the hardships of the long journey behind him had been worth it. Seen even from afar Budapest beckoned him with a magic peculiarly her own.

In Budapest all was splendour, Galty hastened to present a letter of introduction to a great friend of his father, Count Baylor Batoik-Illy. Count Baylor immediately set about arranging entertainments for the young Irish gentleman with the wide, engaging smile and a magnificent appreciation of fine horseflesh. Count Baylor bred the Hator-Orloff strain, beautiful and swift as any horse on earth.

Count Baylor had also bred an extremely beautiful daughter. His daughter and a stallion named Dragoro were the two living things he loved most. In the vaulted banquet hall at Castle Tata-Debrecen hung two huge portraits. One was a life-size painting of Dragoro, black as night. The other was of a tall, slim girl descending the green turf steps of a terrace. Behind her spread an arc of tall ash trees whose massive grey trunks gave great power to the composition of the picture. The girl seemed a dryad emerging from the forest, but a curious dryad, with high cheekbones and slanting, almost Chinese, eyes. There was a look of not-too-well-controlled wildness about the mouth of this arresting face. The mother of Countess Hoja Batoik-Illy was the daughter of a Tartar noble. There was more than a little of the furiously racing Tartar blood in Countess Hoja's veins.

Galty Mallory married Countess Hoja. After a year of travel, they returned to Ireland and settled, if one could ever consider the restless like of Countess Hoja "settled", at Castle Sheela. In any case, she made Galty Mallory a supremely happy man, for he understood and played up to the constant wild adventures which were the breath of life to Countess Hoja

Batoik-Illy Mallory, as she called herself. She bore Galty five children, two daughters and three sons. She was the mother of Ormond Mallory, wild as a hawk and handsome as Lucifer, whom in many other qualities he resembled—pride, for one. It is Ormond Mallory whose ghost now rides the staircase at Castle Sheela on Christmas night, a horseman without a head.

When Ormond Mallory's father died, the boy was eighteen years old. It was a madly dangerous age for a boy with the confused nature of Ormond to have so vast a sum of money at his command. Galty had, as he thought, very wisely provided for just this contingency. He had had no illusions about the waywardness, the arrogant pride of self, and the fiendish temper of the boy. All that was unstable and dross in the Mallory strain, coupled with the tempestuousness of his Tartar forbears, seemed to mingle in the bloodstream of Ormond Mallory. Immediately Galty was buried, Countess Hoja had called Ormond into her sitting-room. She told him that, as the estate was entailed, it must go to him when he reached the age of twenty-one. What she proposed to do now was this: turn over to him at once the actual money that was to come to him. She and the three younger children would go for a long visit to her home in Debrecen. After placing the girls in a convent near Paris, she would return and take up residence at Knockrally, an old Charles II house belonging to the Mallorys at the harbour mouth of Waterford-Old City.

Ormond listened dutifully, albeit nervously, with one eye looking out the window at some of his hounds who were being taught the sport of coursing. His mother's absence would not cause him the slightest sorrow, for nothing in this world mattered to Ormond but Ormond.

As her son turned to leave the room, his mother said, rather bitterly, "The reason for my making this change is this, much as I hate to admit it. The life you are set to lead frightens me. I do not wish to be a party to it. If I felt that I could do anything to stop it, I would try at least. I know I cannot. I have the girls to think of. If they lived in this house, no matter how closely chaperoned by me, they would be tarred by your brush. That is not a pretty picture. I will be blamed by many, I know, for deserting you at your age. But as you are already causing scandal in the village by forcing your attentions on young village girls, I see the way you wish to live, even while I am here. Your father is spared this, at least. It may be partly my fault. Your blood is dark with many crimes from my side of the family. Beware, Ormond, of the village men. However highly placed you may be, they will take their revenge."

Ormond flicked a burr from his leather legging, bowed to his mother, and left the room. Countess Hoja thought to herself she might have spared her breath. Ormond had apparently not heard a word she had said.

Soon after this one-sided interview between Ormond and his mother, during which Ormond had said not one word, Countess Hoja and her two daughters set out for Hungary. Before she left, her second son, Dominic, was placed in a Franciscan school at Lisdoonvarna. Dominic was fifteen years old. He was not nearly so outrageously selfish as his brother Ormond, yet he was rebellious against authority. It was hoped the Franciscans would have a quieting influence. The third boy, last of the Mallory children, died when a small child.

From the moment that Ormond Mallory had Castle Sheela to himself, monarch of all he surveyed, his affairs took a lively turn. For more than a year, he had indulged himself with a rollicking widow who lived in the busy market town of Kilmallock. When Ormond had first met Moira Campbell, she was not a widow, but the predatory young wife of old John Carmichael, a prosperous chemist. When Carmichael died suddenly and was hurriedly buried, a few months after Moira's meeting with the handsome squire of Castle Sheela, ugly rumours flew like October leaves in and out of the doorways of Kilmallock. Moira, behind closed shutters, took stock of her chances. They did not look too bright if she remained in Kilmallock. She sold the chemist's shop and her small house with all her belongings. One month after the death of old John, Moira arrived at the portals of Ormond Mallory's house. She was accompanied by many boxes packed to bursting with new dresses and bonnets provided by the infatuated and generous Ormond.

Moira's arrival was quite open. The old transparent dodge of "housekeeper", so often used by the gentry was spurned by both Moira and the defiant Ormond. She came as his mistress. She might, if her cards told true, end up as his wife.

For a few years we find Ormond occupied mostly with his horses and coursing greyhounds. His knowledge of horses was supreme. As the years passed, he became a power in racing and thoroughbred horse-breeding circles throughout Ireland. However badly Ormond Mallory was regarded by his more conventional neighbours for his loose way of living, men respected him as a fine sportsman. Women secretly envied Mistress Moira, but would have died before admitting it.

Moira Carmichael was a shocking housekeeper. The beautifully chosen furniture, which gave such an air of elegance and comfort to Castle Sheela, was in a sad state of disrepair in no time after her advent. The rooms which had been the talk of the countryside in Brendan Mallory's day were now a shambles. Packs of burr-matted dogs trooped through the suite of drawing-rooms on the first floor. Saddles, spurs, riding-crops, saddle-soap, coursing muzzles, and greasy horse bandages littered every chair and spilled over on to the floor. Fireplaces were never cleaned by the slack servants. Ashes lay in drifts on the floor and were ground into the pale amber rugs by booted feet. Whenever a door or window was opened, clouds of dust swirled through the house. If ever neglect rode wild, it was through the rooms of Castle Sheela.

Cheap, bawdy servants were all that Moira could manage. The decent Irish servitor would not set foot inside the house.

It is told in the village of Galtymore that Countess Hoja, on her return from Hungary, stayed for a while with friends near Castle Sheela. One day she rode over to pay her son a calf. The front door standing open, she walked in. Frozen with amazement and anger at what she saw, the countess started forward to pull the bell cord. Deciding on another course, she walked through the rooms. Cobwebs hung in hammocks from picture frame to candelabrum and swayed back and forth in the breeze from the open door. A thick film of blue-grey dust lay on table tops and mantel shelves. Countess Hoja sailed furiously from room to room, her anger rising at every step. As she came out into the entrance hall, she saw a blowsy, heavy-eyed woman coming slowly down the stairs. It was Moira, newly awakened from sleep. Without a word the Countess Hoja approached the yawning woman and, raising her riding-crop, she dealt Moira a slashing blow across the face. Turning, she walked out of the house.

In the Mallory stables was a young hunter which Ormond called Follow, for the simple reason that even as a foal he would follow Ormond about the demesne very much as a dog will follow the one person he picks out on whom to centre a lifetime of affection and loyalty. Ormond fostered this trick, as he chose to regard it. He showed off Follow to his friends. One day, when Follow was a yearling, Ormond encouraged him to walk up the shallow stone steps leading to the entrance door of the castle. Ormond stood at the top and opened the door. When the young horse had success-fully negotiated the steps, he walked through the door and without hesitation picked his way delicately up the rise of stairs to the door of Ormond's bedroom. This clever trick amused Ormond mightily. Next day he had a runway or ramp built at one side of the stairs. It was built in four broad, shallow rises and enabled Follow to mount the stairs and go down again with ease. At all hours of the day the horse would seek his master in this way. If Ormond was not in his room, Follow would return to the paddock. It came to be such a common sight to see the sleek sorrel horse marching up or down the ramp in the hall of Castle Sheela that no one even noticed. Certainly no one minded.

When Follow was four years old, Ormond started to hunt him with the Limerick Hounds. The horse was a superb mover, took his walls and ditches in a knowledgeable manner, and had a great heart. He endeared himself to the cold, sarcastic Ormond as no human had ever done. It finally got to the point that when Ormond was hunting and the meet was early in the morning, a groom would saddle Follow and the horse would walk out of the stable yard straight to the open front door of the house and march serenely up the ramp to his master's room. Then a little ceremony took place. Ormond would hold an apple in the palm of one hand and stick of sugar in the other. Follow would look first at one delicacy, then the other. Undecided for a moment, he would finally choose. Ormond would then spring into the saddle, and they were off to the meet. For two or three years this was a regular procedure. Moira had raged at the noise made by

Follow's hoofs, of an early morning, on the wooden planking of the ramp. But Moira was gone from Castle Sheela. In the midst of one of her drunken rages, Ormond had packed her off. The last he had heard, she was living with a senile protector in Dublin.

For weeks there had been no one at Castle Sheela save Ormond, the ramping pack of greyhounds and terriers, and the constant visitor, Follow. In Ormond's tireless search for female companionship he roamed the countryside, playing the field. Playing the field spelled danger, the way Ormond did it. Flagrant and ruthless always, his complete disregard for another's feeling was his ultimate undoing.

Among the numerous women to whom Ormond paid marked attention was the boldly handsome but indiscreet wife of a neighbouring landowner, a man so devious in his dealings and of so jealous a nature that at times his actions smacked of madness. One day this man encountered his wife walking with Ormond Mallory in a secluded lane near the gates of Castle Sheela. What took place in this lane is not fully known. Ormond, however, was laid up for months with a broken shoulder.

During these days of enforced idleness, Follow visited Ormond every day. He had another visitor as well—a surprise visitor. His mother, hearing that Moira Carmichael was no longer at the Castle, rode over from Knockrally to stop the night. Ormond was secretly glad to see her, and was charm itself. He even consented to sit for his portrait, which his mother had long wanted him to have done, to hang in the dining-room at Castle Sheela along with portraits of his father and grandfather. An Italian painter named Cannorelli was living in Dublin. Ormond would ask him to pass the tedium of his inactivity. Besides sitting for his portrait, he could brush up on his Italian.

The other request his mother made was that he give a big Christmas party at Castle Sheela, a family party. He must ask his sisters, who had returned from their convent in France and were staying with their mother at Knockrally. Dominic, the brother, could come over for the party from Lisdoonvarna. Ormond told his mother to make whatever arrangements she desired. Countess Hoja returned to Knockrally considering her visit to her son a most successful one.

The portrait of Ormond Mallory was painted and hung "on the line" in the dining-room beside his progenitors. It had a certain dash and fluid grace the other portraits lacked. The picture shows a slender man in his early thirties with a rather highly coloured face, little marred by dissipation. The hair is a light golden brown, unpowdered and tied at the nape of the neck by a wide black ribbon. He wears a dark green coat with silver buttons, and a black stock is loosely tied under the arrogant chin. The eyes arrest you. Cold, insolent, they are the hard steely blue of a winter evening sky. It is an inscrutable face. No one living could ever fathom what Ormond Mallory was thinking. The decoration of the portrait is given great style by a touch of the bizarre. As a compliment to his Hungarian mother,

Ormond had flung over his shoulder a Csikós coat of white wool, heavily braided and embroidered in green, brown, and black.

The Christmas holiday season approached. Castle Sheela was put as much in order as was possible considering the shattered appearance left over from Moira Carmichael's sojourn. The Countess Hoja arrived accompanied by her daughters, Brigid and Caro. When Dominic arrived the afternoon of Christmas Eve, the family party at Castle Sheela was complete.

Late in the evening the Mallorys were sitting before the drawing-room fire. Goblets of light mulled wine were being passed around. Suddenly there was a sound of hoof-beats approaching rapidly along the hard, frosty driveway leading from the entrance gates to the Castle. The horse was pulled up sharply and the sound of an angry voice was heard at the front door demanding of a footman to speak to Ormond Mallory, "Or by the holy God he'll wish he'd never been born!" Apparently Ormond recognised the shouting voice, for, as he hastily rose from his chair by the fire, his mother saw such a look of livid, intense hatred cloud his eyes that it frightened her. "Ormond, what is it? Do you know who that is?" But Ormond had flung out of the room. She heard the front door slam with a force fit to wrench it off its hinges. No more was seen of Ormond that night.

Christmas morning dawned cold and overcast. Follow was the first one up at Castle Sheela. Long before the front door was opened by a sleepy maid, Follow was nuzzling the doorknob, wanting to be let in.

The meet for the Christmas Day hunt was to be held at Rillantora Park, an old abbey, but recently made into a habitable house by Sir John Ainsley, an absentee landlord who had just inherited the place. The house had a dank, broody look even on a bright day. As the straggling riders cantered up to the abbey porch, assembling for the meet, many people shivered in their saddles, almost as much from dread of the house as from the biting wind. Through the densely packed trees of the park, the winter wind soughed and snapped off brittle branches. Horses champed at cold bits, riders banged gloved palms together to restore circulation, red noses ran unheeded. An unease was abroad. Old Lady Clonboy, atop a big raking grey, remarked to a man astride the horse next her, "How Sir John can live in this old shebang is the wonder of the world. The drains are clogged with so much trash left over from the Dark Ages that it defies moving. More murders have been committed in this house than there are chimneys in the roof."

At that moment a late horseman was seen approaching along a narrow ride cut through the trees in the park. It was Ormond Mallory, mounted on Follow. Ormond waved his crop, encompassing the entire group with one greeting. Some waved in return. The hunt moved off. But anyone looking closely at Ormond would have seen that he looked like death. His face was pale and drawn. His eyes shifted to right and left, nervously. His upper lip was puffy and there was a jagged cut at one corner of his mouth.

Christmas Day at Castle Sheela was far from a merry one. All day long there was a tension in the air that affected all within the house. Countess Hoja's neuralgia assailed her, so she kept to her room. Caro and Brigid tried embroidery. No use. Late in the morning they took the terriers for a walk through the old rabbit warrens at the back of the paddock. This kept the girls busy until they returned to join Dominic for a late lunch. Dominic had spent the morning browsing among his father's books in the library. "Too cold to hunt," he said.

In Terrance and Brendan Mallory's day, Christmas dinner at Castle Sheela had been a meal in the great tradition. On this particular Christmas, dinner was set for six o'clock in the evening, with Ormond Mallory presiding at the head of his table.

The day dragged on. Six o'clock came, but no Ormond appeared. Everyone knew the hunt had found its last fox around four o'clock. Dominic had walked out to the gatehouse and talked with the huntsmen returning to Clonboy Castle. They told Dominic they had had a good day.

Mary Corty, the cook, was frantic. Dinner had been ready and waiting to be served these two hours. "It'll be a great ruin, and meself destroyed with the labour," she moaned. Then Kirstey, the maid who had opened the door early that morning for Follow, heard a noise on the stone steps of the entrance porch. It sounded like a heavy body stumbling. Then came the whinnying of a horse, a sobbing kind of whinnying, that of a horse far spent in wind. Kirstey ran to the door and flung it wide open. At the same moment Dominic appeared in the door of the library.

A foundering horse stumbled across the threshold of the hall door. His russet hide was streaked and matted with dried blood and lather.

Astride his back rode horror, the very definition of horror—the body of a man, the legs tied with a rope under the horse's belly, the wrists tied together behind the back. The dark green coat with silver buttons was torn and saturated with blood. Above the collar of this coat there was no head. Ormond Mallory's head had been severed cleanly from his body.

Too stunned by the shock of what they saw to move, Kirstey and Dominic sank back against the wall. Follow, his sides heaving in his last effort, slowly mounted the runway, as he had done daily for years. At the door of his master's bedroom he sank to the floor, dead.

The head of Ormond Mallory was never found, nor was his murderer ever discovered. Jason Fermoy, the neighbouring landowner who had met Ormond in the lane and beaten him with a shillelagh, as Jason later told at the Assizes Court, fell under suspicion and was interrogated by Mr Justice Callahan. Jason proved, beyond doubt, a watertight alibi. He was dismissed. A curious annotation on the margin of this phase of the case, is that, for years after the murder, Mrs Fermoy, heavily veiled, visited the grave of Ormond Mallory in the churchyard at Clonboy. After one of her visits a piece of paper, which she had tucked into a metal flower vase, was disturbed by an errant wind. The paper blew along one of the cemetery paths and was picked up by a lay priest who happened to be passing. Written in heavy black ink on a piece of stiff white paper was this:

EPITAPH

HE WAS WICKED, DESPERATELY WICKED.
BUT HE INVESTED WICKEDNESS
WITH A BRIGHTNESS AND SPARKLE
WHICH MADE IT EXCEEDINGLY ATTRACTIVE.

Soon after his brother Ormond's death, Dominic Mallory went to Italy. There, in Venice, he married a Signorina Lydia Canaletto, niece of the painter whose luminous pictures of the seventeenth-century Venice are world famous. By this marriage Latin blood was infused into the Mallory strain. Countess Hoja died at Knockrally, and the Mallory girls both married Irishmen. It is Caro's great-great-great granddaughter, Mrs Torrance, who now lives at Castle Sheela.

When Dominic brought his Italian bride to Castle Sheela to live, the first thing he did was to remove the wooden ramp constructed by Ormond Mallory to accommodate his equine friend, Follow. But the mere absence of planking does not stop Follow from visiting his master's room as he always did when he was alive. Sometimes, just before dawn, the sound of hoofs hurrying rapidly up a phantom ramp is heard by persons in the house. If they listen they will hear (more sedately now, for the horse bears his master on his back) the iron-shod hoofs going down the ramp. Always on Christmas Day, after darkness has fallen, the front door will open suddenly and slam back against the wall.

Many people say they have seen a ghostly horse and rider mount the shadows beside the stair treads where the ramp used to be. The horse stumbles, as if nearly spent. The swaying rider has no head. Towards sunset on Christmas Day and on Christmas Day only, anyone looking at the portrait of Ormond Mallory, which now hangs over the fireplace in the dining-room, will be rather astonished. A change takes place. The arrogant face with the supercilious mouth is no longer there. Above the black satin stock there is only a dim smudge, which seems to glow with lambent fire. Next morning the painted face is again there, the blue, wintry eyes inscrutable.

In Adversity Be Ye Steadfast

Patrick Boyle

You don't work as a farm labourer for twenty-five solid years, day in, day out, fair weather and foul, without getting to know the peculiarities of your employer. And Andrew McFetridge is a queer duck surely. The neighbours claim he's a dour, thin-lipped Presbyterian, greedy for money and too mean to spend a fluke on the jollifications they themselves indulge in. But that's not the whole of the story. He's certainly a hard-driving boss who'll work the guts out of you from dawn till dusk. Still he won't ask you to do a job he wouldn't tackle himself. And the pay is good. No, all's wrong with the man is that he has a bee in his bonnet about religion.

Now religion is a funny bloody thing. It is a bit like the drink—most people can take it or leave it alone: the odd one becomes an addict. And you can safely describe Andrew as a religious addict. It is his belief—a fundamental article of his faith—that any kind of relaxation is sinful and merits the wrath of God. He neither drinks nor smokes. Never in all his sixty years has he set foot in a dance hall or cinema. In his farmhouse you'll find no such works of the Devil as a radio or a television set. Not even an old-fashioned gramophone. And there's neither chick nor child about the place, although he's married this many a year.

As you'd expect, this way of life does not encourage neighbourly traffic. So the evening when there comes a loud knock at McFetridge's back door, there is a stir out of no one in the kitchen. Andrew, who is sitting at the big

61

open hearth-fire, easing off his wellingtons, stays motionless, one boot held up like a question mark. Over by the dresser, the wife, Jane, stands glowering, a finger to her lips.

There is no second knock. Instead the latch clicks and a man's head is poked round the door. "Evening, folks. Hope we're not intruding."

You'd know at once by the soapy voice and the big black Bible tucked under his oxter that he's one of these travelling preachers. A Holy Roller. Or a Dunker. Or maybe even a Mormon. Without as much as a "by your leave" he comes sailing into the kitchen, followed by his mate, a much smaller man, carrying a class of a leather case.

"Is this where Andrew McFetridge lives?" says the tall man.

Andrew deposits his wellington boot on the floor. "Aye," says he.

"My name is Bryson," the preacher says. "And this," he points, "is a fellow worker in the vineyard of the Lord, Brother Clarke."

Jane is quick off the mark. She clears away the unused dishes, already laid on the bare kitchen table. "We were just sitting down for a mouthful of tea," she says. "You'll maybe join us."

Without waiting for an answer, she gets out the damask table-cloth and the tea-set and the swanky cutlery and the silver teapot—wedding presents kept under lock and key—and she starts setting the table in the new.

"We were told in the village that you were an upright God-fearing Christian, Brother McFetridge," says Bryson.

Jane by now is fluttering around, pulling out chairs from the table. "Will you not sit down?" says she.

"Thank you, Sister," he says. "We just stopped by to see if you would join us in invoking the blessing of the Lord Jesus on both your labours and on ours. A short family prayer session." He gives a pious sort of giggle. "A cup of tea when we are finished would be most welcome."

Andrew frowns. You can see he is embarrassed. "We'd be glad to join you in prayer," he said. "Only –"

Bryson eyes the dishes on the table and the kettle singing on the hob. "We could call back later if we are disturbing you," says he.

"Oh, no," says Andrew. "'Deed you're not disturbing us in any way. It's just that," he jerks his skull as if he were heading a ball, "James here isn't one of us."

"Didn't the Good Lord say, 'In my Father's house are many mansions'? There is shelter for every man, be he Baptist, Presbyterian, Methodist, Anglican –"

"He's a Roman Catholic," says Andrew, as though he's just after donning the black cap.

"No matter," says Bryson. "We are all brethren in Christ, gathered here together to seek the blessings that only heartful prayer can obtain."

"Hallelujah!" says Clarke, the first time he opens his trap.

Andrew clears his throat. "Well, James," says he. "Would you like to join us?"

Would a duck swim? Sure a man would have to be a born idiot to forgo a chance like this. Don't people say that at these prayer meetings they roll about the floor, grinding their teeth? Or go into a fit of the shakes? Or even tear their clothes off? And forby all that, going home now would mean missing up on the tea.

"Och, sure there could be no great harm in saying a mouthful of prayers."

"Very well," says Andrew. "Close over the door, Jane."

As the ould one goes to the door, the cat comes in from the yard, saunters across the kitchen floor and settles down at the fireside. A big brute of a white Persian with its hair trailing the ground, it scowls at the assembled company as though accusing them of trying to hold a religious service in its absence.

Bryson starts leafing through the Bible. "Now, folks," he says, "I am sure there is no need to remind you that if you are seeking help or guidance or consolation, you have only to go to the Book of Psalms. David has the answers to everything. So we will begin with a reading from Psalm 23."

The chairs are pulled back and the company gets to their knees around the kitchen table. For a few seconds the preacher stares up at the ceiling like you'd see a missioner doing in the pulpit, until the coughing and the rustling and the shuffling have died down. At length he starts reading from the Bible.

"The Lord is my shepherd: I shall not want."

A class of an agricultural discourse, no less! The care and rearing of black-faced sheep. Specially laid on for mountainy slobs.

"He maketh me to lie down in green pastures:
He leadeth me beside the still waters."

Green pastures, how are you! And still waters! Little the big fat gulpin knows about herding sheep on the side of a mountain. With grass as scarce as gold dust and waterlogged bog-holes waiting to swallow up the unwary. Not to speak of snow and storm and the depredations of hunting dogs at the dead of night. Oh, 'tis far from the Sperrin Mountains this man of God was reared.

He goes on reading about restoring souls and walking through Death Valley and a lot of other tripe, and then he comes out with:

"Thou preparest a table before me in the
presence of mine enemies."

Believe it or not, those are the preacher's exact words. Not satisfied with persuading a poor bugger to take part in a sectarian gathering, he starts rubbing in the fact that the table you're kneeling beside is laid for the tea and that damn the bite you'll get till they're finished with their bloody ould abracadabra. And on top of everything, reminding you that your enemies are gathered about you, smacking their lips over your plight. Oh, there's no doubt about it, there's little change in this country over the last few hundred years. But what can you do except soldier on and hope that the acrobatics will start before you're destroyed with the hunger.

You'd think he's reading your thoughts, for the next thing he comes out with is:

"I will dwell in the house of the Lord for ever."

And it looks bloody like it, for he closes the Bible and starts a long harangue about the value of prayer. Making contact with the Lord Jesus, he calls it. You would think he's a radio ham the way he talks of switching on the infinite power of the Creator, getting the right wavelength for salvation, tuning in to the Only Begotten Son and babbling away about frequencies and modulations and faulty elements and now and then—cute corbie that he is—getting back again to the sheep farming with the odd reference to slaughtered lambs and wandering sheep and a daft remark about "the mountains skipping like rams, and little hills like lambs". You'd wonder that anyone—let alone a clergyman—could come out with such a load of crap.

Andrew is kneeling up very straight, head askew, face ploughed up into a ferocious frown as though he's having trouble sorting out the meaning of the preacher's words. And no wonder. A mountainy farmer, so thick that he won't give house-room to a wireless set, is hardly likely to make sense out of high frequency prayer. Much less hills lepping around like little lambs.

The ould dolly is crouched over a chair nursing her chin on her clasped hands and gazing into space. Every so often her empty stomach sets up a growling protest that would rouse your sympathy if you weren't feeling worse yourself.

But Brother Bryson must be preaching on a full stomach for he keeps gabbling on, regardless of grumbling guts and scowling faces and dying fire.

At last the sermon ends. But does that conclude the proceedings? No such bloody luck.

"And now, friends," says the preacher, "we will invoke the pity and clemency of our Heavenly Father. And what better way to preface our supplication than the first few verses of Psalm 102?"

He throws back his head, the eyes rolling in their sockets, and addresses the rafters.

"Hear my prayer, O Lord, and let me
come unto Thee.

Hide not Thy face from me in the day
   when I am in trouble:
Incline Thine ear to me: in the day
   when I call answer me speedily."

He has the whole thing off by heart, rattling it out like a nursery rhyme,
only taking an occasional skelly at the open book.

"My heart is smitten, and withered like grass
   so that I forget to eat my bread."

D'you hear that? He has a brass neck on him! Making out that he has
hammered at you with his exhortations till the spit has dried in your
mouth and the hunger gone off you.

"By reason of the voice of my groaning
   my bones cleave to my skin."

Well, you can say that again. The sight of the food on the table and you
kneeling so close is enough to rise turmoil in anyone's guts. Though no
doubt the preacher would claim it is the Word of God that is driving the
burps out of you.

On and on he goes, blethering about pelicans and owls and house-
sparrows; stones and dust and grass; indignation, wrath and drunken
weeping; you could make neither sense nor meaning out of it. 'Twould
put you to sleep instead of giving you the Holy Roller shakes. Indeed,
looking round the company you can see that they are all beginning to show
signs of wear and tear. Jane is yawning her head off. Andrew's eyes are
closed, his head hanging, his body swaying backwards and forwards. He's
flogged out after a hard day's work. And ready for nothing but bed. Even
the cat, sitting up proud as a bloody pasha, is squinting at the dying fire
with drowsy, slitted eyes.

And now Brother Bryson is in full cry. He has closed the Bible and is
waving it aloft, extolling its wisdom and prescience, its reliability as the
answer to all the troubles of the world—fear, loneliness, anxiety, dis-
couragement, sorrow and weariness—its indispensability to the Good Life
and the ultimate crown of salvation, its significance as the corner-stone
of the Christian faith. He drones on, with Brother Clarke chiming in with
an occasional Amen or Hallelujah and the old lady's yawns becoming
more audible and the cat settling down for a comfortable snooze and
Andrew snoring gently as he teeters back and forth, until—

Suddenly his body sags and he slumps forward, his head fetching up
against the table with a crunch that would put the heart across you. The
preacher breaks off in the middle of a sentence. Dead silence for a couple of
seconds.

Then, like a drunken man gathering himself together, Andrew pushes himself back from the table and squats down on his haunches. There is a dazed look on his face and a lump on his forehead the size of a duck egg.

Jane jumps to her feet. "Andrew," she cries, rushing over to him. "Are you badly hurt?"

The two Bible-thumpers join her.

"That's a nasty bump you got, Brother McFetridge," says Bryson.

"Still it didn't draw blood," Clarke says.

Andrew looks at them dully. He draws a hand across his forehead. "Och, 'tis a thing of nothing." The bruise is now as big as an orange.

"He could have split his skull," says Clarke.

"Will you not sit down?" says Bryson pulling up a chair.

"Should I put a poultice on it?" Jane says. "Or would it be as well to get a doctor?"

Andrew eyes them irritably. "What's all the fuss about? Doctors and poultices and sit-down prayer meetings? Over a bit of a clout on the head." He squares his shoulders and draws himself up, clasping his hands together again. You have to hand it to Andrew. No half measures about him. If there's praying to be done, it must be done regimental fashion.

"Maybe there's a bone broken," says Jane. "Or some damage to the —"

"Get down on your knees, woman, and let the Reverend get on with his discourse."

"But you wouldn't mind a poultice? It's only to keep down the swelling."

"Nonsense. I'm as right as the rain."

Fighting words, all right. But the voice is kinda squeaky. And he has gone very pale in the face.

Jane thrusts her hands out in a gesture of despair. "He'll pay no heed to me," she says.

Bryson leaves his Bible down on the table beside a plate of oatcakes that would put you slobbering with the hunger. He turns to Andrew. "Brother McFetridge," he says earnestly. "Our little prayer session is concluded."

Andrew gapes at him stupidly. "Concluded?" he says.

"Yes. We can omit the usual closing hymn."

But Andrew is not taking surrender terms from anyone. Clerical or lay. "Indeed and you will not. Not on my account you won't."

The preacher glances across at the old dolly for guidance, but she shrugs her shoulders helplessly.

"Very well," he says. He clasps his hands and gets in touch with the rafters again. "Abide with us, dear Lord," says he, "for it is towards evening and the day is far spent." He has the neck of a giraffe. If it hadn't been for himself and his butty, the tea would be long since over and the company well on its way to dreamland. "Brother Clarke," he says. "The closing hymn."

Your man grabs the leather case, places it on the dresser and opens it up. A blast of music fills the room, rumbling, thundering, booming. It must be some sort of a recording machine.

Andrew and Jane are listening open-mouthed and out of the tail of an eye you can see the cat standing stiff-legged, its back arched in terror. And why not? For the poor brute, no more than its master and mistress, has no conception of the wonders of amplified music.

The next bloody thing, pandemonium breaks out. A male choir, assisted by the two preachers, are bellowing at the top of their voices "Abide with me: fast falls the eventide".

Above the clamour can be heard the screeching of the cat as, roused to panic, it claws its way up the bricks of the fireplace. Lucky enough, the fire is nearly dead so it comes to no harm. But as it disappears up the chimney, Jane comes to life and starts screaming: "Oh, the cat! The poor cat! It'll be roasted alive."

Andrew is leaning against the table, his hand to his forehead. Bryson, who has been conducting the unseen choir, stands with his hands raised in a papal benediction. Clarke is clutching his mouth as though a note has stuck in his gullet and he's in danger of puking. The machine is still belting out the hymn.

"When other helpers fail, and comforts flee,
Help of the helpless, O abide with me."

Somewhere up the flue of the chimney the cat is howling, the sound muffled but quite audible above the uproar. Jane darts across to the fireplace and, in the lull between verses, calls up, "Pussy! Poor old pussy! Come down, will you. Come down."

Her voice is nearly drowned out with the choir starting up again.

"Swift to its close ebbs out life's little day."

You can hardly blame the bloody cat for staying where it is with all these strange voices bawling out in unison that it's gone closing-time so drink up your drinks don't you know it's after hours the premises must be closed and have you no homes to go to.

The old girl is worried to hell about what's after happening her pet and she starts wringing her hands and shouting blue murder.

"Will somebody do something. Do something will you. Don't just stand there gaping. Do something."

The two preachers rush over to join her and the three of them crouch around the hearth, shouting up the chimney, "Pussy! Pussy! Pussy! Come down, Pussy. Puss! Puss! The naughty puss. Come down, pussy-kins. You can't stay there all night."

Damn the bit heed the cat pays to their exhortations. No more than it does to the mechanised hallions now roaring:

"Through cloud and sunshine, Lord, abide with me."

If the muffled yowling is any indication, the poor brute is up near the chimney-pot by this time, with every intention of abiding there till the coast is clear.

This possibility dawns on Jane, for she straightens up and turns to Bryson. "The roof," she says. "There's nothing for it but the roof."

"How do you mean," says he, "the roof?"

"You'll have to get up on the roof. It's the only way to reach the poor thing."

You can see that Brother Bryson has no stomach for this caper. He starts back-pedalling at once. "Maybe we should try just once more," he says, "to see if it will come down." And then, as an afterthought, "What name do you call it?"

"Eh?" says Jane.

"What name does it answer to?"

"Pussy, of course. Or sometimes Puss."

"Has it no proper name? Like Felix? Or Blanche?"

Jane is getting impatient. "You don't give Christian names to cats. Come on," says she, starting for the door. "I'll show you where the ladder is."

The choir is still going full blast when she comes back into the kitchen but she pays no attention. She makes straight for the fireplace, where she starts calling up the chimney. "Are you there, Pussy? Oh, good! We'll have the poor old puss-cat out of there and safe and sound in a few minutes. There's two good men gone up on the roof to take you down." She swings round. "Isn't that right, Andrew?"

Andrew, hands grasping his knees, is sitting up very straight on a chair. But his face has gone a class of grey and you can hear the clatter of his teeth above the sound of the recording machine.

"What's wrong?" says Jane, dashing over to him.

"I'm cold," says he. "Bitter cold."

She runs a hand across his forehead. "He's done for," she wails. "Och, God help us all, he's done for."

After all these years she should know her husband better. Sure there's only one way you can hurt a tough old cormorant like him and that is through his pocket-book.

"Stop your whining, woman," he says, "and throw a sod or two of turf on the fire."

So away with Jane to the creel at the hearth side where she gathers up an armful of turf and starts building up the fire again, her ears cocked to the chattering teeth of the boss and paying no heed to the crying cat or the noise of the preachers on the roof or the choir bawling:

"I fear no foe with thee at hand to bless."

But the bloody fire won't light and Andrew is getting impatient. "What's keeping you?" he says. "Can you not get the fire going?"

You can see the old birdie is rattled. She glares around, looking for kindling. Spots a bottle on the dresser. Grabs it up and darts back to the fireplace. The screw-top seems to be jammed and as she is struggling to release it a voice is heard from the chimney. It is Brother Clarke. "I can't reach far enough," says he. "You'd better try."

You can hear them shuffling about on the roof. Changing places carefully. And then Bryson's voice. Very clear. As though he has his big head poked into the chimney-pot.

"I see the little fellow. There should be no trouble getting him out."

Just then Andrew lets a groan out of him. Not a groan of pain, but of irritation. He has come to the realisation, not for the first time, that you must do everything yourself. That a woman can never be trusted to handle anything. He tries to ease himself off the chair. "Here," he says, "give me that bottle."

But Jane has been roused to a flurry of action. The top of the bottle is off. She is splashing the contents wildly over the dying fire.

It must be petrol she is using for suddenly there is a WHOOOOOOSH, and a sheet of flame rushes up the chimney. After that it is pure bloody bedlam. From the old dolly a scream. From the roof-top a roar of pain, ending in what sounds awful like a well-known expletive. From the cat in the chimney a muffled howl, mounting to a screech as it loses its grip and tumbles down the flue, to land, tail ablaze, in the hearth.

For a split second it crouches there, blazing tail threshing back and forth. Then, like a shot off a shovel, it starts careering around the room. You know how the squib they call the Jumping Jenny behaves when you light it—leaping madly around and banging against walls and furniture. Well, that's the way the cat is performing, only now and then it starts whirling around with the sparks flying off it as though it is giving an imitation of a Catherine wheel. The long hairs of the Persian breed make ideal bonfire fuel, so by the time it dashes out the open door into the yard, screeching blue murder, the poor brute is ablaze from stem to stern.

The company is too stunned to make a move or say a word. But overhead you can hear Clarke's awestricken voice: "Hey, look at the cat! It's on fire!"

Between grunts and moans, Bryson can be heard casting doubts on its ancestry and expressing an unChristian disregard for its ultimate fate. These sentiments seem to rouse Jane from her stupor, for she starts rushing to the door. "My God!" she says. "The poor creature!"

She is soon pulled to a halt.

"The table-cloth, woman!"

It is Andrew. He has struggled to his feet and is pointing with out-stretched hand. He appears excited. And who would blame him. In its fiery exit, the cat must have brushed against the table-cloth. Now the draught from the open door is just starting to set alight the smouldering material. It is confined to a single fold of the cloth and anyone with half an ounce of wit could quench it with a clap of the hand. But Jane, the poor slob, yanks the cloth and its precious burden off the table and, in her excitement, stamps and grinds and tramples it into submission on the floor.

You would nearly find it in your heart to feel sorry for Andrew. There he stands, a look of horror on his face as the full extent of the catastrophe dawns on him. A pedigree tea-set, cutlery of the best, a damask table-cloth and a valuable silver teapot, the only surviving relics of the past, maybe never before put to use, now lying smashed and damaged and scattered on the kitchen floor. Not to mention that he is going weak in the knees and the cold sweat is rising on him and the lump on his head is still swelling from the bang he got only now it has started throbbing like an old-fashioned threshing-machine and he is so hungry that he'd eat his way through two ends of a dunghill and he is dog-tired after a hard day's work and if every-one would only go home he would clear off to bed and he wishes to goodness that the choir would lower their voices a little for it is driving him com-pletely crackers. Mouth open, he is about to make his protest when the commotion starts up overhead. The two preachers are banging on the roof-tiles and bellowing at the top of their voices "Fire! Fire! Fire!"

Andrew stumbles to the kitchen door and you can hear his gasp as he realises that his hay barn is ablaze. The flames are roaring up sky-high and you can hear the hiss and crackle as the fire spreads through the tightly packed hay. Above the sound of the fire, and like a class of an accompani-ment, the choir is chanting:

"Hold Thou Thy cross before my closing eyes,
Shine through the gloom and point me to the skies."

You would think they were deliberately making a mock of poor Andrew's reaction to this final catastrophe. For in the glare from the fire you can see him leaning against the doorpost with his eyes closed as though he doesn't want to see what is happening. It is a cruel sight, to say nothing but the truth. Jane is over at the pump in the middle of the yard, her arm going like a fiddler's elbow as she drives the pump up and down. The two preachers have collected buckets and are running backwards and forwards, shouting encouragement to each other as they try to throw water on the flames. With the heat, they cannot get near enough for the water to reach the fire. But even if it did, it would have as much effect as the squirt of a tobacco spit.

The fire has a right hold now over the whole hay barn and in its light you can see the bruise on Andrew's forehead pulsing and his lips murmuring. You'd gamble the last tosser in your pocket that what he is muttering about is the undesirability of house-cats, the crass stupidity of wives, the doubtful value of travelling preachers to the evangelical cause, and the folly of carrying thrift to the point of refusing to insure your hay barn against fire. You would be very wrong. For if you incline your ear close, you will hear him repeating fervently in time with the choir:

"In life, in death, O Lord, abide with me."

Michael and Mary

Seamus O'Kelly

Mary had spent many days gathering wool from the whins on the
headland. They were the bits of wool shed by the sheep before the
shearing. When she had got a fleece that fitted the basket she took
it down to the canal and washed it. When she had done washing, it was a
soft, white, silky fleece. She put it back in the brown sally basket, pressing
it down with her long, delicate fingers. She had risen to go away, holding
the basket against her waist, when her eyes followed the narrow neck of
water that wound through the bog.

She could not follow the neck of yellow water very far. The light of day
was failing. A haze hung over the great Bog of Allen that spread out level
on all sides of her. The boat loomed out of the haze on the narrow neck of
the canal water. It looked, at first, a long way off, and it seemed to come in
a cloud. The soft rose light that mounted the sky caught the boat and bur-
nished it like dull gold. It came leisurely, drawn by the one horse, looking
like a Golden Barque in the twilight. Mary put her brown head a little to
one side as she watched the easy motion of the boat. The horse drew himself along deliberately, the patient head going up and down with every
heavy step. A crane rose from the bog, flapping two lazy wings across the
wake of the boat, and, reaching its long neck before it, got lost in the haze.

The figure that swayed by the big arm of the tiller on the Golden Barque
was vague and shapeless at first, but Mary felt her eyes following the slow
movements of the body. Mary thought it was very beautiful to sway by

the arm of the tiller, steering a Golden Barque through the twilight.

Then she realised suddenly that the boat was much nearer than she thought. She could see the figures of the men plainly, especially the slim figure by the tiller. She could trace the rope that slackened and stretched taut as it reached from the boat to the horse. Once it splashed the water, and there was a little sprout of silver. She noted the whip looped under the arm of the driver. Presently she could count every heavy step of the horse, and was struck by the great size of the shaggy fetlocks. But always her eyes went back to the figure by the tiller.

She moved back a little way to see the Golden Barque pass. It came from a strange, far-off world, and having traversed the bog went away into another unknown world. A red-faced man was sitting drowsily on the prow. Mary smiled and nodded to him, but he made no sign. He did not see her; perhaps he was asleep. The driver who walked beside the horse had his head stooped and his eyes on the ground. He did not look up as he passed. Mary saw his lips moving, and heard him mutter to himself; perhaps he was praying. He was a shrunken, misshaped little figure and kept step with the brute in the journey over the bog. But Mary felt the gaze of the man by the tiller upon her. She raised her eyes.

The light was uncertain and his peaked cap threw a shadow over his face. But the figure was lithe and youthful. He smiled as she looked up, for she caught a gleam of his teeth. Then the boat had passed. Mary did not smile in return. She had taken a step back and remained there quietly. Once he looked back and awkwardly touched his cap, but she made no sign.

When the boat had gone by some way she sat down on the bank, her basket of wool beside her, looking at the Golden Barque until it went into the gloom. She stayed there for some time, thinking long in the great silence of the bog. When at last she rose, the canal was clear and cold beneath her. She looked into it. A pale new moon was shining down in the water.

Mary often stood at the door of the cabin on the headland and watching the boats that crawled like black snails over the narrow streak of water through the bog. But they were not all like black snails now. There was a Golden Barque among them. Whenever she saw it she smiled, her eyes on the figure that stood by the shaft of the tiller.

One evening she was walking by the canal when the Golden Barque passed. The light was very clear and searching. It showed every plank, battered and tar-stained, on the rough hulk, but for all that it lost none of its magic for Mary. The little shrunken driver, head down, the lips moving, walked beside his horse. She heard his low mutters as he passed. The red-faced man was stooping over the side of the boat, swinging out a vessel tied to a rope, to haul up some water. He was singing a ballad in a monotonous voice. A tall, dark, spare man was standing by the funnel, looking vacantly ahead. Then Mary's eyes travelled to the tiller.

Mary stepped back with some embarrassment when she saw the face. She backed into a hawthorn that grew all alone on the canal bank. It was covered with bloom. A shower of the white petals fell about her when she stirred the branches. They clung about her hair like a wreath. He raised his cap and smiled. Mary did not know the face was so eager, so boyish. She smiled a little nervously at last. His face lit up, and he touched his cap again.

The red-faced man stood by the open hatchway going into the hold, the vessel of water in his hand. He looked at Mary and then at the figure beside the tiller.

"Eh, Michael?" the red-faced man said quizzically. The youth turned back to the boat, and Mary felt the blush spreading over her face.

"Michael!"

Mary repeated the name a little softly to herself. The gods had delivered up one of their great secrets.

She watched the Golden Barque until the two square slits in the stern that served as portholes looked like two little Japanese eyes. Then she heard a horn blowing. It was the horn they blew to apprise lock-keepers of the approach of a boat. But the nearest lock was a mile off. Besides, it was a long, low sound the horn made, not the short, sharp, commanding blast they blew for lock-keepers. Mary listened to the low sound of the horn, smiling to herself. Afterwards the horn always blew like that whenever the Golden Barque was passing the solitary hawthorn.

Mary thought it was very wonderful that the Golden Barque should be in the lock one day that she was travelling with her basket to the market in the distant village. She stood a little hesitantly by the lock. Michael looked at her, a welcome in his eyes.

"Going to Bohermeen?" the red-faced man asked.

"Ay, to Bohermeen," Mary answered.

"We could take you to the next lock," he said, "it will shorten the journey. Step in."

Mary hesitated as he held out a big hand to help her to the boat. He saw the hesitation and turned to Michael. "Now, Michael," he said.

Michael came to the side of the boat, and held out his hand. Mary took it and stepped on board. The red-faced man laughed a little. She noticed that the dark man who stood by the crooked funnel never took his eyes from the stretch of water before him. The driver was already urging the horse to his start on the bank. The brute was gathering his strength for the pull, the muscles standing out on his haunches. They glided out of the lock.

It was half a mile from one lock to another. Michael had bidden her stand beside him at the tiller. Once she looked up at him and she thought the face shy but very eager, the most eager face that ever came across the bog from the great world.

Afterwards, whenever Mary had the time, she would make a cross-cut through the bog to the lock. She would step in and make the mile journey with Michael on the Golden Barque. Once, when they were journeying together, Michael slipped something into her hand. It was a quaint trinket, and shone like gold.

"From a strange sailor I got it," Michael said.

Another day that they were on the barque, the blinding sheets of rain that often swept over the bog came upon them. The red-faced man and the dark man went into the hold. Mary looked about her, laughing. But Michael held out his great waterproof for her. She slipped into it and he folded it about her. The rain pelted them, but they stood together, Michael holding the big coat folded about her. She laughed a little nervously. "You will be wet," she said.

Michael did not answer. She saw the eager face coming down close to hers. She leaned against him a little and felt the great strength of his arms about her. They went sailing away together in the Golden Barque through all the shining seas of the gods.

"Michael," Mary said once, "is it not lovely?"

"The wide ocean is lovely," Michael said. "I always think of the wide ocean going over the bog."

"The wide ocean!" Mary said with awe. She had never seen the wide ocean. Then the rain passed. When the two men came up out of the hold Mary and Michael were standing together by the tiller.

Mary did not go down to the lock after that for some time. She was working in the reclaimed ground on the headland. Once the horn blew late in the night. It blew for a long time, very softly and lowly. Mary sat up in bed listening to it, her lips parted, the memory of Michael on the Golden Barque before her. She heard the sound dying away in the distance. Then she lay back on her pillow, saying she would go down to him when the Golden Barque was on the return journey.

The figure that stood by the tiller on the return was not Michael's. When Mary came to the lock the red-faced man was telling out the rope, and where Michael always stood by the tiller there was the short figure of a man with a pinched, pock-marked face.

When the red-faced man wound the rope round the stump at the lock, bringing the boat to a standstill, he turned to Mary. "Michael is gone voyaging," he said.

"Gone voyaging?" Mary repeated.

"Ay," the man answered. "He would be always talking to the foreign sailors in the dock where the canal ends. His eyes would be upon the big masts of the ships. I always said he would go."

Mary stood there while the Golden Barque was in the lock. It looked like a toy ship packed in a wooden box.

"A three-master he went in," the red-faced man said, as they made ready for the start. "I saw her standing out for the sea last night, Michael is under the spread of big canvas. He had the blood in him for the wide ocean, the wild blood of the rover." And the red-faced man, who was the boss of the boat, let his eyes wander up the narrow neck of water before him.

Mary watched the Golden Barque, moving away, the grotesque figure standing by the tiller. She stayed there until a pale moon was shining below her, turning over a little trinket in her fingers. At last she dropped it into the water.

It made a little splash, and the vision of the crescent was broken.

Going into Exile

Liam O'Flaherty

Patrick Feeney's cabin was crowded with people. In the large kitchen men, women and children lined the walls, three deep in places, sitting on forms, chairs, stools, and on one another's knees. On the cement floor three couples were dancing a jig and raising a quantity of dust, which was, however, soon sucked up the chimney by the huge turf fire that blazed on the hearth. The only clear space in the kitchen was the corner to the left of the fireplace, where Pat Mullaney sat on a yellow chair, with his right ankle resting on his left knee, a spotted red handkerchief on his head that reeked with perspiration, and his red face contorting as he played a tattered old accordian. One door was shut and the tins hanging on it gleamed in the firelight. The opposite door was open and over the heads of the small boys that crowded in it and outside it, peering in at the dancing couples in the kitchen, a starry June sky was visible and, beneath the sky, shadowy grey crags and misty, whitish fields lay motionless, still and sombre. There was a deep, calm silence outside the cabin and within the cabin, in spite of the music and dancing in the kitchen and the singing in the little room to the left, where Patrick Feeney's eldest son Michael sat on the bed with three other young men, there was a haunting melancholy in the air.

The people were dancing, laughing and singing with a certain forced and boisterous gaiety that failed to hide from them the real cause of their being there, dancing singing and laughing. For the dance was on account of Patrick Feeney's two children, Mary and Michael, who were going to the United States on the following morning.

Feeney himself, a black-bearded, red-faced, middle-aged peasant, with white ivory buttons on his blue frieze shirt and his hands stuck in his leather waist belt, wandered restlessly about the kitchen, urging the people to sing and dance, while his mind was in agony all the time, thinking that on the following day he would lose his two eldest children, never to see them again perhaps. He kept talking to everybody about amusing things, shouted at the dancers and behaved in a boisterous and abandoned manner. But every now and then he had to leave the kitchen, under the pretence of going to the pigsty to look at a young pig that was supposed to be ill. He would stand, however, upright against his gable and look gloomily at some star or other, while his mind struggled with vague and peculiar ideas that wandered about in it. He could make nothing at all of his thoughts, but a lump always came up his throat, and he shivered, although the night was warm.

Then he would sigh and say with a contraction of his neck, "Oh, it's a queer world this and no doubt about it. So it is." Then he would go back to the cabin again and begin to urge on the dance, laughing, shouting and stamping on the floor.

Towards dawn, when the floor was crowded with couples, arranged in fours, stamping on the floor and going to and fro, dancing the "Walls of Limerick", Feeney was going out to the gable when his son Michael followed him out. The two of them walked side by side about the yard over the grey sea pebbles that had been strewn there the previous day. They walked in silence and yawned without need, pretending to be taking the air. But each of them was very excited, Michael was taller than his father and not so thickly built, but the shabby blue serge suit that he had bought for going to America was too narrow for his broad shoulders and the coat was too wide around the waist. He moved clumsily in it and his hands appeared altogether too bony and big and red, and he didn't know what to do with them. During his twenty-one years of life he had never worn anything other than the homespun clothes of Inverara, and the shop-made clothes appeared as strange to him and as uncomfortable as a dress suit worn by a man working in a sewer. His face was flushed a bright red and his blue eyes shone with excitement. Now and again he wiped the perspiration from his forehead with the lining of his grey tweed cap.

At last Patrick Feeney reached his usual position at the gable end. He halted, balanced himself on his heels with his hands in his waist belt, coughed and said, "It's going to be a warm day." The son came up beside him, folded his arms and leaned his right shoulder against the gable.

"It was kind of Uncle Ned to lend the money for the dance, Father," he said. "I'd hate to think that we'd have to go without something or other, just the same as everybody else has. I'll send you that money the very first money I earn, Father . . . even before I pay Aunt Mary for my passage money. I should have all that money paid off in four months, and then I'll have some more money to send you by Christmas."

And Michael felt very strong and manly recounting what he was going to do when he got to Boston, Massachusetts. He told himself that with his great strength he would earn a great deal of money. Conscious of his youth and his strength and lusting for adventurous life, for the moment he forgot the ache in his heart that the thought of leaving his father inspired in him.

The father was silent for some time. He was looking at the sky with his lower lip hanging, thinking of nothing. At last he sighed as a memory struck him. "What is it?" said the son. "Don't weaken, for God's sake. You will only make it hard for me." "Fooh!" said the father suddenly with pretended gruffness. "Who is weakening? I'm afraid that your new clothes make you impudent." Then he was silent for a moment and continued in a low voice, "I was thinking of that potato field you sowed alone last spring the time I had influenza. I never set eyes on the man that could do it better. It's a cruel world that takes you away from the land that God made you for."

"Oh, what are you talking about, Father?" said Michael irritably. "Sure what did anybody ever get out of the land but poverty and hard work and potatoes and salt?"

"Ah yes," said the father with a sigh, "but it's your own, the land, and over there"—he waved his hand at the western sky—"'you' be giving your sweat to some other man's land, or what's equal to it."

"Indeed," muttered Michael, looking at the ground with a melancholy expression in his eyes, "it's poor encouragement you are giving me."

They stood in silence fully five minutes. Each hungered to embrace the other, to cry, to beat the air, to scream with excess of sorrow. But they stood silent and sombre, like nature about them, hugging their woe. Then they went back to the cabin. Michael went into the little room to the left of the kitchen, to the three young men who fished in the same currach with him and were his bosom friends. The father walked into the large bedroom to the right of the kitchen.

The large bedroom was also crowded with people. A large table was laid for tea in the centre of the room and about a dozen young men were sitting at it, drinking tea and eating buttered raisin cake. Mrs Feeney was bustling about the table, serving the food and urging them to eat. She was assisted by her two younger daughters and by another woman, a relative of her own. Her eldest daughter Mary, who was going to the United States that day, was sitting on the edge of the bed with several other young women. The bed was a large four-poster bed with a deal canopy over it, painted red, and the young women were huddled together on it. So that there must have been about a dozen of them there. They were Mary Feeney's particular friends, and they stayed with her in that uncomfortable position just to show how much they liked her. It was a custom.

Mary herself sat on the edge of the bed with her legs dangling. She was a pretty, dark-haired girl of nineteen, with dimpled, plump, red cheeks and ruminative brown eyes that seemed to cause little wrinkles to come and go in her little low forehead. Her nose was soft and small and rounded. Her mouth was small and the lips were red and open. Beneath her white blouse that was frilled at the neck and her navy blue skirt that outlined her limbs as she sat on the edge of the bed, her body was plump, soft, well-moulded and in some manner exuded a feeling of freshness and innocence. So that she seemed to have been born to be fondled and admired in luxurious surroundings instead of having been born a peasant's daughter, who had to go to the United States that day to work as a servant or maybe in a factory.

And as she sat on the edge of the bed crushing her little handkerchief between her palms, she kept thinking feverishly of the United States, at one moment with fear and loathing, at the next with desire and longing. Unlike her brother she did not think of the work she was going to do or the money that she was going to earn. Other things troubled her, things of which she was half-ashamed, half-afraid, thoughts of love and of foreign men and of clothes and of houses where there were more than three rooms and where people ate meat every day. She was fond of life, and several young men among the local gentry had admired her in Inverara. But. . . .

She happened to look up and she caught her father's eyes as he stood silently by the window with his hands stuck in his waist belt. His eyes rested on hers for a moment and then he dropped them without smiling, and with his lips compressed he walked down into the kitchen. She shuddered slightly. She was a little afraid of her father, although she knew that he loved her very much and he was very kind to her. But the winter before he had whipped her with a dried willow rod, when he caught her one evening behind Tim Hernon's cabin after nightfall, with Tim Hernon's son Bartly's arms around her waist and he kissing her. Ever since, she always shivered slightly when her father touched her or spoke to her.

"Oho!" said an old peasant who sat at the table with a saucer full of tea in his hand and his grey flannel shirt open at his thin, hairy, wrinkled neck. "Oho! Indeed, but it's a disgrace to the island of Inverara to let such a beautiful woman as your daughter go away, Mrs Feeney. If I were a young man, I'd be flayed alive if I'd let her go."

There was a laugh and some of the women on the bed said, "Bad cess to you, Patsy Coyne, if you haven't too much impudence, it's a caution." But the laugh soon died. The young men sitting at the table felt embarrassed and kept looking at one another sheepishly, as if each tried to find out if the others were in love with Mary Feeney.

"Oh, well, God is good," said Mrs Feeney, as she wiped her lips with the tip of her bright, clean, check apron. "What will be must be, and sure there is hope from the sea, but there is no hope from the grave. It is sad and the poor have to suffer, but. . . ." Mrs Feeney stopped suddenly, aware that all these platitudes meant nothing whatsoever. Like her husband she was unable to think intelligently about her two children going away. Whenever the reality of their going away, maybe for ever, three thousand miles into a vast unknown world, came before her mind, it seemed that a thin bar of some hard metal thrust itself forward from her brain and rested behind the wall of her forehead. So that almost immediately she became stupidly conscious of the pain caused by the imaginary bar of metal and she forgot the dread prospect of her children going away. But her mind grappled with the things about her busily and efficiently, with the preparation of food, with the entertaining of her guests, with the numerous little things that have to be done in a house where there is a party and which only a woman can do properly. These little things, in a manner, saved her, for the moment at least, from bursting into tears whenever she looked at her daughter and whenever she thought of her son, whom she loved most of all her children, because perhaps she nearly died giving birth to him and he had been very delicate until he was twelve years old. So she laughed down in her breast a funny laugh she had that made her heave where her check apron rose out from the waist band in a deep curve. "A person begins to talk," she said with a shrug of her shoulders sideways, "and then a person says foolish things."

"That's true," said the old peasant, noisily pouring more tea from his cup to his saucer.

But Mary knew by her mother laughing that way that she was very near being hysterical. She always laughed that way before she had one of her fits of hysterics. And Mary's heart stopped beating suddenly and then began again at an awful rate as her eyes became acutely conscious of her mother's body, the rotund, short body with the wonderful mass of fair hair growing grey at the temples and the fair face with the soft liquid brown eyes, that grew hard and piercing for a moment as they looked at a thing and then grew soft and liquid again, and the thin-lipped small mouth with the beautiful white teeth and the deep perpendicular grooves in the upper lip and the tremor that always came in the corner of the mouth, with love, when she looked at her children. Mary became acutely conscious of all these little points, as well as of the little black spot that was on her left breast below the nipple and the swelling that came now and again in her legs and caused her to have hysterics and would one day cause her death. And she was stricken with horror at the thought of leaving her mother and at the selfishness of her thoughts. She had never been prone to thinking of anything important but now, somehow for a moment, she had a glimpse of her mother's life that made her shiver and hate herself as a cruel, heartless, lazy, selfish wretch. Her mother's life loomed up before her eyes, a life of continual misery and suffering, hard work, birth pangs, sickness and again hard work and hunger and anxiety. It loomed up and then it fled again, a little mist came before her eyes and she jumped down from the bed, with the jaunty twirl of her head that was her habit when she set her body in motion.

"Sit down for a while, Mother," she whispered, toying with one of the black ivory buttons on her mother's brown bodice. "I'll look after the table." "No, no," murmured the mother with a shake of her whole body, "I'm not a bit tired. Sit down, my treasure. You have a long way to travel today."

And Mary sighed and went back to the bed again.

At last somebody said, "It's broad daylight." And immediately everybody looked out and said, "So it is, and may God be praised." The change from the starry night to the grey, sharp dawn was hard to notice until it had arrived. People looked out and saw the morning light sneaking over the crags, silently, along the ground, pushing the mist banks upwards. The stars were growing dim. A long way off invisible sparrows were chirping in their ivied perch in some distant hill or other. Another day had arrived and even as the people looked at it, yawned and began to search for their hats, caps and shawls preparing to go home, the day grew and spread its light and made things move and give voice. Cocks crew, blackbirds carolled, a dog let loose from a cabin by an early riser chased madly after an imaginary robber, barking as if his tail were on fire. The people said goodbye and began to stream forth from Feeney's cabin. They were going to their homes to see to the morning's work before going to Kilmurrage to see the emigrants off on the steamer to the mainland. Soon the cabin was empty except for the family.

All the family gathered into the kitchen and stood about for some minutes talking sleepily of the dance and of the people who had been present. Mrs Feeney tried to persuade everybody to go to bed, but everybody refused. It was four o'clock and Michael and Mary would have to set out for Kilmurrage at nine. So tea was made and they all sat about for an hour drinking it and eating raisin cake and talking. They only talked of the dance and of the people who had been present.

There were eight of them there, the father and mother and six children. The youngest child was Thomas, a thin boy of twelve, whose lungs made a singing sound every time he breathed. The next was Bridget, a girl of fourteen, with dancing eyes and a habit of shaking her short golden curls every now and then for no apparent reason. Then there were the twins, Julia and Margaret, quiet, rather stupid, flat-faced girls of sixteen. Both their upper front teeth protruded slightly and they were both great workers and very obedient to their mother. They were all sitting at the table, having just finished a third large pot of tea, when suddenly the mother hastily gulped down the remainder of the tea in her cup, dropped the cup with a clatter to her saucer and sobbed once through her nose.

"Now Mother," said Michael sternly, "what's the good of this work?"

"No, you are right, my pulse," she replied quietly. "Only I was just thinking how nice it is to sit here surrounded by all my children, all my little birds in my nest, and then two of them going to fly away made me sad." And she laughed, pretending to treat it as a foolish joke.

"Oh, that be damned for a story," said the father, wiping his mouth on his sleeve; "there's work to be done. You Julia, go and get the horse.

Margaret, you milk the cow and see that you give enough milk to the calf this morning." And he ordered everybody about as if it were an ordinary day of work.

But Michael and Mary had nothing to do and they sat about miserably conscious that they had cut adrift from the routine of their home life. They no longer had any place in it. In a few hours they would be homeless wanderers. Now that they were cut adrift from it, the poverty and sordidness of their home life appeared to them under the aspect of comfort and plenty.

So the morning passed until breakfast-time at seven o'clock. The morning's work was finished and the family was gathered together again. The meal passed in a dead silence. Drowsy after the sleepless night and conscious that the parting would come in a few hours, nobody wanted to talk. Everybody had an egg for breakfast in honour of the occasion. Mrs Feeney, after her usual habit, tried to give her egg first to Michael, then to Mary, and as each refused it, she ate a little herself and gave the remainder to little Thomas who had the singing in his chest. Then the breakfast was cleared away. The father went to put the creels on the mare so as to take the luggage into Kilmurrage. Michael and Mary got the luggage ready and began to get dressed. The mother and the other children tidied up the house. People from the village began to come into the kitchen, as was customary, in order to accompany the emigrants from their home to Kilmurrage.

At last everything was ready. Mrs Feeney had exhausted all excuses for moving about, engaged on trivial tasks. She had to go into the big bedroom where Mary was putting on her new hat. The mother sat on a chair by the window, her face contorting on account of the flood of tears she was keeping back. Michael moved about the room uneasily, his two hands knotting a big red handkerchief behind his back. Mary twisted about in front of the mirror that hung over the black wooden mantelpiece. She was spending a long time with the hat. It was the first one she had ever worn, but it fitted her beautifully, and it was in excellent taste. It was given to her by the schoolmistress, who was very fond of her, and she herself had taken it in a little. She had an instinct for beauty in dress and deportment.

But the mother, looking at how well her daughter wore the cheap navy blue costume and the white frilled blouse, and the little round black hat with a fat, fluffy, glossy curl covering each ear, and the black silk stockings with blue clocks in them, and the little black shoes that had laces of three colours in them, got suddenly enraged with. . . . She didn't know with what she got enraged. But for the moment she hated her daughter's beauty, and she remembered all the anguish of giving birth to her and nursing her and toiling for her, for no other purpose than to lose her now and let her go away, maybe to be ravished wantonly because of her beauty and her love of gaiety. A cloud of mad jealousy and hatred against this impersonal beauty that she saw in her daughter almost suffocated the mother, and she stretched out her hands in front of her unconsciously and then just as suddenly her anger vanished like a puff of smoke, and she burst into wild tears, wailing, "My children, oh, my children, far over the sea you will be carried from me, your mother." And she began to rock herself and she threw her apron over her head.

Immediately the cabin was full of the sound of bitter wailing. A dismal cry rose from the women gathered in the kitchen. "Far over the sea they will be carried," began woman after woman, and they all rocked themselves and hid their heads in their aprons. Michael's mongrel dog began to howl on the hearth. Little Thomas sat down on the hearth beside the dog and, putting his arms around him, he began to cry, although he didn't know exactly why he was crying, but he felt melancholy on account of the dog howling and so many people being about.

In the bedroom the son and daughter, on their knees, clung to their mother, who held their heads between her hands and rained kisses on both heads ravenously. After the first wave of tears she had stopped weeping. The tears still ran down her cheeks, but her eyes gleamed and they were dry. There was a fierce look in them as she searched all over the heads of her two children with them, with her brows contracted, searching with a fierce terror-stricken expression, as if by the intensity of her stare she hoped to keep a living photograph of them before her mind. With her quivering lips she made a queer sound like "im-m-m-m" and she kept kissing. Her right hand clutched at Mary's left shoulder and with her left she fondled the back of Michael's neck. The two children were sobbing freely. They must have stayed that way a quarter of an hour.

Then the father came into the room, dressed in his best clothes. He wore a new frieze waistcoat, with a grey and black front and a white back. He held his soft black felt hat in one hand and in the other he had a bottle of holy water. He coughed and said in a weak gentle voice that was strange to him, as he touched his son, "Come now, it is time."

Mary and Michael got to their feet. The father sprinkled them with holy water and they crossed themselves. Then, without looking at their mother, who lay in the chair with her hands clasped on her lap, looking at the ground in a silent tearless stupor, they left the room. Each hurriedly kissed little Thomas, who was not going to Kilmurrage, and then, hand in hand, they left the house. As Michael was going out the door he picked a piece of loose whitewash from the wall and put it in his pocket. The people filed out after them, down the yard and on to the road, like a funeral procession. The mother was left in the house with little Thomas and two old peasant women from the village. Nobody spoke in the cabin for a long time.

Then the mother rose and came into the kitchen. She looked at the women, at her little son and at the hearth, as if she were looking for something she had lost. Then she threw her hands into the air and ran out into the yard. "Come back," she screamed. "Come back to me."

She looked wildly down the road with dilated nostrils, her bosom heaving. But there was nobody in sight. Nobody replied. There was a crooked stretch of limestone road, surrounded by grey crags that were scorched by the sun. The road ended in a hill and then dropped out of sight. The hot June day was silent. Listening foolishly for an answering cry, the mother imagined she could hear the crags simmering under the hot rays of the sun. It was something in her head that was singing.

The two old women led her back into the kitchen. "There is nothing that time will not cure," said one. "Yes. Time and patience," said the other.

Cords

Edna O'Brien

E verything was ready, the suitcase closed, her black velvet coat collar carefully brushed, and a list pinned to the wall reminding her husband when to feed the hens and turkeys, and what foodstuffs to give them. She was setting out on a visit to her daughter Claire in London, just like any mother, except that *her* daughter was different: she'd lost her faith, and she mixed with queer people and wrote poems. If it was stories one could detect the sin in them, but these poems made no sense at all and therefore seemed more wicked. Her daughter had sent the money for the air ticket. She was going now, kissing her husband goodbye, tender towards him in a way that she never was, throughout each day, as he spent his time looking through the window at the wet currant bushes, grumbling about the rain, but was in fact pleased at the excuse to hatch indoors, and asked for tea all the time, which he lapped from a saucer, because it was more pleasurable.

"The turkeys are the most important," she said, kissing him goodbye, and thinking far-away to the following Christmas, to the turkeys she would sell, and the plumper ones she would give as gifts.

"I hope you have a safe flight," he said. She'd never flown before.

"All Irish planes are blessed, they never crash," she said, believing totally in the God that created her, sent her this venial husband, a largish farmhouse, hens, hardship, and one daughter who'd changed, become moody, and grown away from them completely.

The journey was pleasant once she'd got over the shock of being strapped down for the take-off. As they went higher and higher she looked out at the very white, wispish cloud and thought of the wash-tub and hoped her husband would remember to change his shirt while she was away. The trip would have been perfect but that there was a screaming woman who had to be calmed down by the air hostess. She looked like a woman who was being sent to a mental institution, but did not know it.

Claire met her mother at the airport and they kissed warmly, not having seen each other for over a year.

"Have you stones in it?" Claire said, taking the fibre suitcase. It was doubly secured with a new piece of binding twine. Her mother wore a black straw hat with clusters of cherries on both sides of the brim.

"You were great to meet me," the mother said.

"Of course I'd meet you," Claire said, easing her mother right back on the taxi seat. It was a long ride and they might as well be comfortable.

"I could have navigated," the mother said, and Clare said "nonsense" a little too brusquely. Then to make amends she asked gently how the journey was.

"Oh I must tell you, there was this very peculiar woman and she was screaming."

Claire listened and stiffened, remembering her mother's voice that became low and dramatic in a crisis, the same voice that said "Sweet Lord your father will kill us", or "What's to become of us, the bailiff is here", or "Look, look, the chimney is on fire".

"But otherwise?" Claire said. This was a holiday, not an expedition into the past.

"We had tea and sandwiches. I couldn't eat mine, the bread was buttered."

"Still faddy?" Claire said. Her mother got bilious if she touched butter, fish, olive oil, or eggs; although her daily diet was mutton stew, or home-cured bacon.

"Anyhow, I have nice things for you," Claire said. She had bought in stocks of biscuits, jellies and preserves because these were the things her mother favoured, these foods that she herself found distasteful.

The first evening passed well enough. The mother unpacked the presents —a chicken, bread, eggs, a tapestry of a church spire which she'd done all winter, stitching at it until she was almost blind, a holy water font, ashtrays made from shells, lamps converted from bottles, and a picture of a matador assembled by sticking small varnished pebbles on to hardboard.

Claire laid them along the mantelshelf in the kitchen, and stood back, not so much to admire them as to see how incongruous they looked, piled together.

"Thank you," she said to her mother, as tenderly as she might have when she was a child. These gifts touched her, especially the tapestry, although it was ugly. She thought of the winter nights and the Aladdin lamp smoking (they expected the electricity to be installed soon), and her mother hunched over her work, not even using a thimble to ease the needle through, because she believed in sacrifice, and her father turning to say, "Could I borrow your glasses, Mam, I want to have a look at the paper?" He was too lazy to have his own eyes tested and believed that his wife's glasses were just as good. She could picture them at the fire night after night, the turf flames green and fitful, the hens locked up, foxes prowling around in the wind, outside.

"I'm glad you like it, I did it specially for you," the mother said gravely, and they both stood with tears in their eyes, savouring those seconds of tenderness, knowing that it would be short-lived.

"You'll stay seventeen days," Claire said, because that was the length an economy ticket allowed. She really meant, "Are you staying seventeen days?"

"If it's all right," her mother said over humbly. "I don't see you that often, and I miss you."

Claire withdrew into the scullery to put on the kettle for her mother's hot-water bottle; she did not want any disclosures now, any declaration about how hard life had been and how near they'd been to death during many of the father's drinking deliriums.

"Your father sent you his love," her mother said, nettled because Claire had not asked how he was.

"How is he?"

"He's great now, never touches a drop."

Claire knew that if he had, he would have descended on her, the way he used to descend on her as a child when she was in the convent, or else she would have had a telegram, of clipped urgency, "Come home. Mother".

"It was God did it, curing him like that," the mother said.

Claire thought bitterly that God had taken too long to help the thin frustrated man who was emaciated, crazed and bankrupted by drink. But she said nothing, she merely filled the rubber bottle, pressed the air from it with her arm, and then conducted her mother upstairs to bed.

Next morning they went up to the centre of London and Claire presented her mother with fifty pounds. The woman got flushed and began to shake her head, the quick uncontrolled movements resembling those of a beast with the staggers.

"You always had a good heart, too good," she said to her daughter, as her eyes beheld racks of coats, raincoats, skirts on spinning hangers, and all kinds and colours of hats.

"Try some on," Claire said. "I have to make a phone call."

There were guests due to visit her that night—it had been arranged weeks before—but as they were Bohemian people, she could not see her mother suffering them, or them suffering her mother. There was the added complication that they were a "trio"—one man and two women; his wife and his mistress. At that point in their lives the wife was noticeably pregnant.

On the telephone the mistress said they were looking forward, awfully, to the night, and Claire heard herself substantiate the invitation by saying she had simply rung up to remind them. She thought of asking another man to give a complexion of decency to the evening, but the only three unattached men she could think of had been lovers of hers and she could not call on them; it seemed pathetic.

"Damn," she said, irritated by many things, but mainly by the fact that she was going through one of those bleak, loveless patches that come in everyone's life, but, she imagined, came more frequently the older one got. She was twenty-eight. Soon she would be thirty. Withering.

"How do?" her mother said in a ridiculous voice when Claire returned. She was holding a hand mirror up to get a back view of a ridiculous hat, which she had tried on. It resembled the shiny straw she wore for her trip, except that it was more ornamental and cost ten guineas. That was the second point about it that Claire noted. The white price tag was hanging over the mother's nose. Claire hated shopping the way other people might hate going to the dentist. For herself she never shopped. She merely saw things in windows, ascertained the size, and bought them.

"Am I too old for it?" the mother said. A loaded question in itself.

"You're not," Claire said. "You look well in it."

"Of course I've always loved hats," her mother said, as if admitting to some secret vice. Claire remembered drawers with felt hats laid into them, and bobbins on the brims of hats, and little aprons of veiling, with spots which, as a child, she thought might crawl over the wearer's face.

"Yes, I remember your hats," Claire said, remembering too the smell of empty perfume bottles and camphor, and a saxe blue hat that her mother once got on approbation, by post, and wore to mass before returning it to the shop.

"If you like it, take it," Claire said indulgently.

The mother bought it, along with a reversible raincoat and a pair of shoes. She told the assistant who measured her feet about a pair of shoes which lasted her for seventeen years, and were eventually stolen by a tinker-woman, who afterwards was sent to jail for the theft.

"Poor old creature I wouldn't have wished jail on her," the mother said, and Claire nudged her to shut up. The mother's face flushed under the shelter of her new, wide-brimmed hat.

"Did I say something wrong?" she said as she descended uneasily on the escalator, her parcels held close to her.

"No, I just thought she was busy, it isn't like shops at home," Claire said.

"I think she was enjoying the story," her mother said, gathering courage before she stepped off, on to the ground floor.

At home they prepared the food and the mother tidied the front room before the visitors arrived. Without a word she carried all her own trophies

—the tapestry, the pebble picture, the ashtrays, the holy water font and the other ornaments—and put them in the front room alongside the books, the pencil drawings and the poster of Bengal that was a left-over from Claire's dark-skinned lover.

"They're nicer in here," the mother said, apologising for doing it, and at the same time criticising the drawing of the nude.

"I'd get rid of some of those things if I were you," she said in a serious tone to her daughter.

Claire kept silent, and sipped the whiskey she felt she needed badly. Then to get off the subject she asked after her mother's feet. They were fixing a chiropodist appointment for the next day.

The mother had changed into a blue blouse, Claire into velvet pants, and they sat before the fire on low pouffes with a blue-shaded lamp casting a restful light on their very similar faces. At sixty, and made up, the mother still had a poem of a face: round, pale, perfect and with soft eyes, expectant, in spite of what life had brought. On the whites there had appeared blobs of green, the sad green of old age.

"You have a tea-leaf on your eyelid," she said to Claire, putting up her hand to brush it away. It was mascara which got so smeared that Claire had to go upstairs to repair it.

At that precise moment the visitors came.

"They're here," the mother said when the hall bell shrieked.

"Open the door," Claire called down.

"Won't it look odd, if you don't do it?" the mother said.

"Oh, open it," Claire called impatiently. She was quite relieved that they would have to muddle through their own set of introductions.

The dinner went off well. They all liked the food and the mother was not as shy as Claire expected. She told about her journey, but kept the "mad woman" episode out of it, and about a television programme she'd once seen, showing how bird's nest soup was collected. Only her voice was unnatural.

After dinner Claire gave her guests enormous brandies, because she felt relieved that nothing disastrous had been uttered. Her mother never drank spirits of course.

The fulfilled guests sat back, sniffed brandy, drank their coffee, laughed, tipped their cigarette ash on the floor, having missed the ashtray by a hair's breadth, gossiped, and refilled their glasses. They smiled at the various new ornaments but did not comment, except to say that the tapestry was nice.

"Claire likes it," the mother said timidly, drawing them into another silence. The evening was punctuated by brief but crushing silences.

"You like Chinese food then?" the husband said. He mentioned a restaurant which she ought to go and see. It was in the East End of London and getting there entailed having a motor car.

"You've been there?" his wife said to the young blonde mistress who had hardly spoken.

"Yes and it was super except for the pork which was drowned in Chanel Number Five. Remember?" she said, turning to the husband, who nodded.

"We must go some time," his wife said. "If ever you can spare an evening." She was staring at the big brandy snifter that she let rock back and forth in her lap. It was for rose petals but when she saw it she insisted on drinking from it. The petals were already dying on the mantelshelf.

"That was the night we found a man against a wall, beaten up," the mistress said, shivering, recalling how she had actually shivered.

"You were so sorry for him," the husband said, amused.

"Wouldn't anyone be?" the wife said tartly, and Claire turned to her mother and promised that they would go to that restaurant the following evening.

"We'll see," the mother said. She knew the places she wanted to visit: Buckingham Palace, the Tower of London and the waxworks museum. When she went home it was these places she would discuss with her neighbours who'd already been to London, not some seamy place where men were flung against walls.

"No, not another, it's not good for the baby," the husband said, as his wife balanced her empty glass on the palm of her hand and looked towards the bottle.

"Who's the more important, me or the baby?"

"Don't be silly, Marigold," the husband said.

"Excuse me," she said in a changed voice. "Whose welfare are you thinking about?" She was on the verge of an emotional outburst, her cheeks flushed from brandy and umbrage. By contrast Claire's mother had the appearance of a tombstone, chalk white and deadly still.

"How is the fire?" Claire said, staring at it. On that cue her mother jumped up and sailed off with the coal-scuttle.

"I'll get it," Claire said, following. The mother did not even wait until they reached the kitchen.

"Tell me," she said, her blue eyes pierced with insult, "which of those two ladies is he married to?"

"It's not your concern," Claire said, hastily. She had meant to smooth it over, to say that the pregnant woman had some mental disturbance, but instead she said hurtful things about her mother being narrow-minded and cruel.

"Show me your friends and I know who you are," the mother said and went away to shovel the coal. She left the filled bucket outside the living-room door and went upstairs. Claire, who had gone back to her guests, heard the mother's footsteps climbing the stairs and going into the bedroom overhead.

"Is your mother gone to bed?" the husband asked.

"She's tired I expect," Claire said, conveying weariness too. She wanted them to go. She could not confide in them even though they were old friends. They might sneer. They were not friends any more than the ex-lovers, they were all social appendages, extras, acquaintances cultivated in order to be able to say to other acquaintances, "Well one night a bunch of us went mad and had a nude sit-in. . . ." There was no one she trusted, no one she could produce for her mother and feel happy about it.

"Music, brandy, cigarettes. . . ." They were recalling her, voicing their needs, wondering who would go to the machine for the cigarettes. Pauline did. They stayed until they'd finished the packet, which was well after midnight.

Claire hurried to her mother's room and found her awake with the light on, fingering her horn rosary beads. The same old black ones.

"I'm sorry," Claire said.

"You turned on me like a tinker," her mother said, in a voice cracked with emotion.

"I didn't mean to," Claire said. She tried to sound reasonable, assured; she tried to tell her mother that the world was a big place and contained many people, all of whom held various views about various things.

"They're not sincere," her mother said, stressing the last word.

"And who is?" Claire said, remembering the treacherous way the lovers vanished, or how former landladies rigged meters so that units of electricity cost double. Her mother had no notion of how lonely it was to read manuscripts all day, and write a poem once in a while, when one became consumed with a memory or an idea, and then to constantly go out, seeking people, hoping that one of them might fit, might know the shorthand of her, body and soul.

"I was a good mother, I did everything I could, and this is all the thanks I get." It was spoken with such justification that Claire turned and laughed, hysterically. An incident leaped to her tongue, something she had never recalled before.

"You went to hospital," she said to her mother, "to have your toe lanced, and you came home and told me, *me*, that the doctor said 'Raise your right arm until I give you an injection', but when you did, he gave you no injection, he just cut into your toe. Why did you tell it?" The words fell out of her mouth unexpectedly, and she became aware of the awfulness when she felt her knees shaking.

"What are you talking about?" her mother said numbly. The face that was round, in the evening, had become old, twisted, bitter.

"Nothing," Claire said. Impossible to explain. She had violated all the rules: decency, kindness, caution. She would never be able to laugh it off in the morning. Muttering an apology she went to her own room and sat on her bed, trembling. Since her mother's arrival every detail of her childhood kept dogging her. Her present life, her work, the friends she had, seemed insubstantial compared with all that had happened before. She could count the various batches of white, hissing geese—it was geese in those days—that wandered over the swampy fields, one year after another, hid in memory she could locate the pot-holes on the driveway where rain lodged, and where leaking oil from a passing car made rainbows. Looking down into rainbows to escape the colour that was in her mind, or on her tongue. She'd licked four fingers once that were slit by an unexpected razor blade which was wedged upright in a shelf where she'd reached to find a sweet, or to finger the secret dust up there. The same colour had been on her mother's violated toe underneath the big, bulky bandage. In chapel too, the sanctuary light was a bowl of blood with a flame laid into it. These images did not distress her at the time. She used to love to slip into the chapel, alone, in the daytime, moving from one Station of the Cross to the next, being God's exclusive pet, praying that she would die before her mother did, in order to escape being the scapegoat of her father. How could she have known, how could any of them have known that twenty years later, zipped into a heated, plastic tent, treating herself to a steam bath she would suddenly panic and cry out convinced that her sweat became as drops of blood. She put her hands through the flaps and begged the masseuse to protect her, the way she had begged her mother, long ago. Made a fool of herself. The way she made a fool of herself with the various men. The first night she met the Indian she was wearing a white fox collar, and its whiteness under his dark, well-chiselled chin made a stark sight as they walked through a mirrored room to a table, and saw, and were seen, in mirrors. He said something she couldn't hear.

"Tell me later," she said, already putting her little claim on him, already saying, "You are not going to abandon me in this room of mirrors, in my bluish-white fox that so complements your bluish-black lips." But after a few weeks he left, like the others. She was familiar with the various tactics of withdrawal—abrupt, honest, nice. Flowers, notes posted from the provinces, and the "I don't want you to get hurt" refrain. They reminded her of the trails that slugs leave on a lawn in summer mornings, the sad, silver trails of departure. Their goings were far more vivid than their comings, or was she only capable of remembering the worst? Remembering everything, solving nothing. She undressed, she told herself that her four fingers had healed, that her mother's big toe was now like any other person's big toe, that her father drank tea and held his temper, and that one day she would meet a man whom she loved and did not frighten away. But it was brandy optimism. She'd gone down and carried the bottle up. The brandy gave her hope but it disturbed her heart beats and she was unable to sleep. As morning approached she rehearsed the sweet and conciliatory things she would say to her mother.

They went to mass on Sunday, but it was obvious that Claire was not in the habit of going: they had to ask the way. Going in, her mother took a small liqueur bottle from her handbag and filled it with holy water from the font. "It's always good to have it," she said to Claire, but in a bashful way. The outburst had severed them, and they were polite now in a way that should never have been.

After mass they went—because the mother had stated her wishes—to the waxworks museum, saw the Tower of London and walked across the park that faced Buckingham Palace.

"Very good grazing here," the mother said. Her new shoes were getting spotted from the damp, highish grass. It was raining. The spokes of the mother's umbrella kept tapping Claire's, and no matter how far she drew away, the mother moved accordingly, to prong her, it seemed.

"You know," the mother said. "I was thinking."

Claire knew what was coming. Her mother wanted to go home; she was worried about her husband, her fowls, the washing that would have piled up, the spring wheat that would have to be sown. In reality she was miserable. She and her daughter were farther away now than when they wrote letters each week and discussed the weather, or work, or the colds they'd had.

"You're only here six days," Claire said. "And I want to take you to the theatre and restaurants. Don't go."

"I'll think about it," the mother said. But her mind was made up.

Two evenings later they waited in the airport lounge, hesitant to speak, for fear they might miss the flight number.

"The change did you good," Claire said. Her mother was togged out in new clothes and looked smarter. She had two more new hats in her hand, carrying them in the hope they would escape the notice of the customs men.

"I'll let you know if I have to pay duty on them," she said.

"Do," Claire said, smiling, straightening her mother's collar, wanting to say something endearing, something that would atone, without having to go over their differences, word for word.

"No one can say but that you fitted me out well, look at all my style," the mother said smiling at her image in the glass door of the telephone box. "And our trip up the river," she said, "I think I enjoyed it more than anything." She was referring to a short trip they'd taken down the Thames to Westminster. They had planned to go in the opposite direction towards the greenness of Kew and Hampton Court but they'd left it—at least Claire had left it—too late and could only go towards the city on a passenger boat that was returning from those green places.

Claire had been miserly with her time and on that particular evening she'd sat at her desk pretending to work, postponing the time until she got up and rejoined her mother, who was downstairs sewing on all the buttons that had fallen off over the years. And now the mother was thanking her, saying it had been lovely. Lovely. They had passed warehouses and cranes brought to their evening standstill yellow and tilted, pylons like floodlit honeycombs in the sky, and boats, and gasworks, and filthy chimneys. The spring evening had been drenched with sewerage smell and yet her mother went on being thankful.

"I hope my mad lady won't be aboard," the mother said, trying to make a joke out of it now.

"Not likely," Claire said, but the mother declared that life was full of strange and sad coincidences. They looked at each other, looked away, criticised a man who was wolfing sandwiches from his pocket, looked at the airport clock and compared the time on their watches.

"Sssh . . . ssh . . ." Claire had to say.

"That's it," they both said then, relieved. As if they had secretly feared the flight number would never be called.

At the barrier they kissed, their damp cheeks touched and stayed for a second like that, each registering the other's sorrow.

"I'll write to you, I'll write oftener," Claire said, and for a few minutes she stood there waving, weeping, not aware that the visit was over and that she could go back to her own life now, such as it was.

Christmas in London

William Trevor

You always looked back, she thought. You looked back at other years, other Christmas cards arriving, the children younger. There was the year Patrick had cried, disliking the holly she was decorating the living-room with. There was the year Bridget had got a speck of coke in her eye on Christmas Eve and had to be taken to the hospital at Hammersmith in the middle of the night. There was the first year of their marriage, when she and Dermot were still in Waterford. And ever since they'd come to London there was the presence on Christmas Day of their landlord, Mr Joyce, a man whom they had watched becoming elderly.

She was middle-aged now, with touches of grey in her fluffy black hair, easy in her cheerfulness, running a bit to fat. Her husband was the opposite : thin and seeming ascetic, with more than a hint of the priest in him, a good man. "Will we get married, Norah?" he'd said one night in the Tara Ballroom in Waterford, 6 November 1949. The proposal had astonished her. It was his brother Ned, bulky and fresh-faced, a different kettle of fish altogether, whom she'd been expecting to make it.

Patiently he held a chair for her while she strung paper-chains across the room, from one picture-rail to another. He warned her to be careful about attaching anything to the electric light, and still held the chair while she put sprigs of holly behind the pictures. He was cautious by nature and alarmed by little things, particularly anxious in case she fell off chairs. He'd never mount a chair himself, to put up decorations or anything else: he'd be useless at it in his opinion and it was his opinion that mattered. He'd never been able to do a thing about the house but it didn't matter because since the boys had grown up they'd been able to attend to whatever she couldn't manage herself. You wouldn't dream of remarking on it: he was the way he was, considerate and thoughtful in what he did do, teetotal, clever, full of fondness for herself and for the family they'd reared, full of respect for her also.

"Isn't it remarkable how quick it comes round, Norah?" he said, both hands still gripping the back of the chair. "Isn't it no time since last year?"

"No time at all."

"Though a lot happened in the year, Norah."

"An awful lot happened."

Two of the pictures she decorated were scenes of Waterford: the quays, and a man driving sheep past the Bank of Ireland. Her mother had given them to her, taking them down from the hall of the farmhouse. There was a gilt-framed picture of the Virgin and Child and other, smaller pictures. She placed her last sprig of holly, a piece with berries on it, above the Virgin's halo.

"I'll make a cup of tea," she said, descending from the chair and smiling at him.

"A cup of tea'd be great, Norah."

The living-room contained three brown armchairs and a mahogany table with upright chairs around it, and a sideboard with a television set on it. It was crowded by this furniture and seemed even smaller than it was because of the decorations that had been added. On the mantelpiece, above a built-in gas fire, Christmas cards were arrayed on either side of a green clock, ornate in a nineteen-thirties style.

The house was in a terrace in Fulham. It had always been too small for the family, but now that Patrick and Brendan no longer lived there things were easier. Patrick had married a girl called Pearl six months ago, almost as soon as his period of training with the Midland Bank had ended. Brendan was training in Liverpool, with a firm of computer manufacturers. The three remaining children were still at school, Bridget at the nearby convent, Cathal and Tom at the Sacred Heart Primary. When Patrick and Brendan had moved out, the room they'd always shared had become Bridget's. Until then Bridget had slept in her parents' room and she'd have to return there this Christmas because Brendan would be back for three nights. Patrick and Pearl would just come for Christmas Day. They'd be going to Pearl's people, in Croydon, on Boxing Day—St Stephen's Day, as Norah and Dermot always called it, in the Irish manner.

"It'll be great, having them all," he said. "A family again, Norah."

"And Pearl."

"She's part of us now, Norah."

"Will you have biscuits with your tea? I have a packet of Nice."

He said he would, thanking her. He was a meter-reader with North Thames Gas, a position he had held for twenty-five years, ever since he'd emigrated. In Waterford he'd worked as a clerk in the Customs, not earning very much and not much caring for the stuffy, smoke-laden office he shared with half a dozen other clerks. He had come to England because Norah had thought it was a good idea, because she'd always wanted to work in a London shop. She'd been given a job in Dickens and Jones, in the dress materials department, and he'd begun the life of a meter-reader, cycling from door to door, remembering the different houses and where the meters were situated in each, being agreeable to householders: all of it suited him from the start. He devoted time to thought while he rode about, and in particular to thought about religious matters.

In her small kitchen she made the tea and carried it on a tray into the living-room. She'd been late this year with the decorations. She always liked to get them up a week in advance because they set the mood, making everyone feel right for Christmas. She'd been busy with stuff for a stall Father Malley had asked her to run for his Christmas Sale. A fashion stall he'd called it, but not quite knowing what he meant she'd just asked people for any old clothes they had, jumble really. Because of the time it had taken she hadn't had a minute to see to the decorations until this afternoon, two days before Christmas Eve. But that, as it turned out, had been all for the best. Bridget and Cathal and Tom had gone over to Hammersmith to the pictures. Dermot didn't work on a Monday afternoon: it was convenient that they'd have an hour or two alone together because there was the matter of Mr Joyce to bring up. Not that she wanted to bring it up, but it couldn't be just left there.

"The cup that cheers," he said, breaking a biscuit in half. Deliberately she put off raising a subject that was unpleasant. She watched him nibbling the biscuit and then dropping three heaped spoons of sugar into his tea and stirring it. He loved tea. The first time he'd taken her out, to the Savoy in Waterford, they'd had tea afterwards in the cinema café and they'd talked about the film and about people they knew. He'd come to live in Waterford from the country, from the farm his brother had inherited, quite close to her father's farm. He reckoned he'd settled, he told her that night: Waterford wasn't sensational, but it suited him in a lot of ways. If he hadn't married her he'd still be there, working eight hours a day in the Customs and not caring for it, yet managing to get by because he had his religion to assist him.

"Did we get a card from Father Jack yet?" he inquired, referring to a distant cousin, a priest in Chicago.

"Not yet. But it's always on the late side, Father Jack's. It was February last year."

She sipped her tea, sitting in one of the other brown armchairs, on the other side of the gas fire. It was pleasant being alone with him in the decorated room, the green clock ticking on the mantelpiece, the Christmas cards, dusk gathering outside. She smiled and laughed, taking another biscuit while he lit a cigarette. "Isn't this great?" she said. "A bit of peace for ourselves?"

Solemnly he nodded.

"Peace comes dropping slow," he said, and she knew he was quoting from some book or other. Quite often he said things she didn't understand. "Peace and goodwill," he added, and she understood that all right.

He tapped the ash from his cigarette into an ashtray which was kept for his use, beside the gas fire. All his movements were slow. He was a slow thinker, even though he was clever. He arrived at a conclusion, having thought long and carefully; he balanced everything in his mind. "We must think about that, Norah," he'd said that day, twenty-five years ago, when she'd suggested that they should move to England. A week later he'd said that if she really wanted to he'd agree.

They talked about Bridget and Cathal and Tom. When they came in from the cinema they'd only just have time to change their clothes before setting out again for the Christmas party at Bridget's convent.

"It's a big day for them. Let them lie in in the morning, Norah."

"They could lie in for ever." She laughed, in case there might seem to be harshness in this recommendation. With Christmas excitement running high the less she heard from them the better, she said, laughing again.

"Did you get Cathal the gadgets he wanted?"

"Chemistry stuff. A set in a box."

"You're great the way you manage, Norah."

She denied that. She poured more tea for both of them. She said, as casually as she could, "Mr Joyce won't come. I'm not counting him in for Christmas Day."

"He hasn't failed us yet, Norah."

"He won't come this year." She smiled through the gloom at him. "I think we'd best warn the children about it."

"Where would he go if he didn't come here? Where'd he get his dinner?"

"Lyons used to be open in the old days."

"He'd never do that."

"The Bulrush Café has a turkey dinner advertised. There's a lot of people go in for that now. If you have a mother doing a job maybe she hasn't the time for the cooking. They go out to a hotel or a café, three or four pounds a head. . . ."

"Mr Joyce wouldn't go to a café. No one could go into a café on their own on a Christmas Day."

"He won't come here, dear."

It had to be said: it was no good just pretending, laying a place for the old man on an assumption that had no basis to it. Mr Joyce would not come because Mr Joyce, last August, had ceased to visit them. Every Friday night he used to come, for a cup of tea and a chat, to watch the nine o'clock news with them. Every Christmas Day he'd brought carefully chosen presents for the children and chocolates and nuts and cigarettes. He'd given Patrick and Pearl a radio as a wedding present.

"I think he'll come all right. I think maybe he hasn't been too well. God help him, it's a great age, Norah."

"He hasn't been ill, Dermot."

Every Friday Mr Joyce had sat there in the third of the brown armchairs, watching the television, his bald head inclined so that his good ear was closer to the screen. He was tallish, rather bent now, frail and bony, with a modest white moustache. In his time he'd been a builder, which was how he had come to own property in Fulham, a self-made man who'd never married. That evening in August he had been quite as usual. Bridget had kissed him good-night because for as long as she could remember she'd always done that when he came to sit in the living-room. He'd asked Cathal how he was getting on with his afternoon paper-round.

There had never been any difficulties over the house. They considered that he was fair in his dealings with them; they were his tenants and his friends. When the Irish bombed English people to death in Birmingham and Guildford he did not cease to arrive on Friday evenings and on Christmas Day. The bombings were discussed after the news, the Tower of London bomb, the bomb in the bus, and all the others. "Maniacs," Mr Joyce said and nobody contradicted him.

"He would never forget the children, Norah, Not at Christmas."

His voice addressed her from the shadows. She felt the warmth of the gas fire reflected in her face and knew if she looked in a mirror she'd see that she was quite flushed. Dermot's face never reddened. Even though he was nervy, he never displayed emotion. On all occasions his face retained its paleness, his eyes acquired no glimmer of passion. No wife could have a better husband, yet in the matter of Mr Joyce he was so wrong it almost frightened her.

"Is it tomorrow I call in for the turkey?" he said.

She nodded, hoping he'd ask her if anything was the matter because as a rule she never just nodded in reply to a question. But he didn't say anything. He stubbed his cigarette out. He asked if there was another cup of tea in the pot.

"Dermot, would you take something round to Mr Joyce?"

"A message, is it?"

"I have a tartan tie for him."

"Wouldn't you give it to him on the day, Norah? Like you always do." He spoke softly, still insisting. She shook her head.

It was all her fault. If she hadn't said they should go to England, if she hadn't wanted to work in a London shop, they wouldn't be caught in the trap they'd made for themselves. Their children spoke with London accents. Patrick and Brendan worked for English firms and would make their homes in England. Patrick had married an English girl. They were Catholics and they had Irish names, yet home for them was not Waterford.

"Could you make it up with Mr Joyce, Dermot? Could you go round with the tie and say you were sorry?"

"Sorry?"

"You know what I mean." In spite of herself her voice had acquired a trace of impatience, an edginess that was unusual in it. She did not ever speak to him like that. It was the way she occasionally spoke to the children.

"What would I say I was sorry for, Norah?"

"For what you said that night." She smiled, calming her agitation. He lit another cigarette, the flame of the match briefly illuminating his face. Nothing had changed in his face. He said:

"I don't think Mr Joyce and I had any disagreement, Norah."

"I know, Dermot. You didn't mean anything –"

"There was no disagreement, girl."

There had been no disagreement, but on that evening in August something else had happened. On the nine o'clock news there had been a report of another outrage and afterwards, when Dermot had turned the television off, there'd been the familiar comment on it. He couldn't understand the mentality of people like that, Mr Joyce had yet again remarked, people killing just anyone, destroying life for no reason. Dermot had shaken his head over it, she herself had said it was uncivilised. Then Dermot had added that they mustn't of course forget what the Catholics in the North had suffered. The bombs were a crime but it didn't do to forget that the crime would not be there if generations of Catholics in the North had not been treated as animals. There'd been a silence then, a difficult kind of silence that she'd broken herself. All that was in the past, she'd said hastily, in a rush. Nothing in the past or the present, nothing at all, could justify the killing of innocent people. Even so, Dermot had added, it didn't do to avoid the truth. Mr Joyce had not said anything.

"I'd say there was no need to go round with the tie, Norah. I'd say he'd make the effort on Christmas Day."

"Of course he won't." Her voice was raised, with more than impatience in it now. But her anger was controlled. "Of course he won't come."

"It's a time for goodwill, Norah. Another Christmas: to remind us."

He spoke slowly, the words prompted by some interpretation of God's voice in answer to a prayer: she recognised that in his deliberate tone.

Miserably she said, not wishing to say it, "It isn't just another Christmas. It's an awful kind of Christmas. It's a Christmas to be ashamed of and you're making it worse, Dermot." Her lips were trembling in a way that was uncomfortable. If she tried to calm herself she'd become jittery instead, she might even begin to cry. Mr Joyce had been generous and tactful, she said loudly. It made no difference to Mr Joyce that they were Irish people, that their children went to school with the children of I.R.A. men. Yet his generosity and his tact had been thrown back in his face. Everyone knew that the Catholics in the North had suffered, that generations of injustice had been twisted into the shape of a cause. But you couldn't say it to an old man who had hardly been outside Fulham in his life. You couldn't say it because when you did it sounded like an excuse for murder.

"You have to state the truth, Norah. It's there to be told."

"I never yet cared for a North of Ireland person, Catholic or Protestant. Let them fight it out and not bother us."

"You shouldn't say that, Norah."

"It's more of your truth for you."

He didn't reply. There was the gleam of his face for a moment as he drew on his cigarette. In all their married life they had never had a quarrel that was in any way serious, yet she felt herself now in the presence of a seriousness that was too much for her. She had told him that whenever a new bombing took place she prayed it might be the work of the Angry Brigade, or any group that wasn't Irish. She'd told him that in shops she'd begun to feel embarrassed because of her Waterford accent. He'd said she must have courage, and she realised now that he had drawn on courage himself when he'd made the remark to Mr Joyce. He would have prayed and considered before making it. He would have seen it in the end as his Catholic duty.

"He thinks you don't condemn people being killed." She spoke quietly even though she felt a wildness inside her. She felt she should be out on the streets, shouting in her Waterford accent, violently stating that the bombers were more despicable with every breath they drew, that hatred and death were all they deserved. She saw herself on Fulham Broadway, haranguing the passers-by, her greying hair blown in the wind, her voice more passionate than it had ever been before. But none of it was the kind of thing she could do because she was not that kind of woman. She hadn't the courage, any more than she had the courage to urge her anger to explode in their living-room. For all the years of her marriage there had never been the need of such courage before: she was aware of that, but found no consolation in it.

"I think maybe he's seen it by now," he said, "how one thing leads to another."

She felt insulted by the words. She willed on herself the strength to shout, to pour out a torrent of fury at him, but the strength did not come. Standing up, she stumbled in the gloom and felt a piece of holly under the sole of her shoe. She turned the light on.

"I'll pray that Mr Joyce will come," he said.

She looked at him, pale and thin, with his priestly face. For the first time since he had asked her to marry him in the Tara Ballroom she did not love him. He was cleverer than she was, yet he seemed half-blind. He was good, yet he seemed hard in his goodness, as though he'd be better without it. Up to the very last moment on Christmas Day there would be the pretence that their landlord might arrive, that God would answer a prayer because His truth had been honoured. She considered it hypocrisy, unable to help herself in that opinion.

He talked but she did not listen. He spoke of keeping faith with their own, of being a Catholic. Crime begot crime, he said: God wanted it to be known that one evil led to another. She continued to look at him while he spoke, pretending to listen but wondering instead if in twelve months' time, when another Christmas came, he would still be cycling from house to house to read gas meters. Or would people have objected, requesting a meter-reader who was not Irish? An objection to a man with an Irish accent was down-to-earth and ordinary. It didn't belong in the same grand category as crime begetting crime or God wanting something to be known, or in the category of truth and conscience. In the present circumstances the objection would be understandable and fair. It seemed even right that it should be made, for it was a man with an Irish accent in whom the worst had been brought out by the troubles that had come, who was guilty of a cruelty no one would have believed him capable of. Their harmless elderly landlord might die in the course of that same twelve months, a friendship he had valued not made up, his last Christmas lonely. Grand though it might seem in one way, all of it was petty.

Once, as a girl, she would have cried, but her contented marriage had caused her to lose that habit. She cleared up the tea things, reflecting that the bombers would be pleased if they could note the victory they'd scored in a living-room in Fulham. And on Christmas Day, when a family sat down to a conventional meal, the victory would be greater. There would be crackers and chatter and excitement, the Queen and the Pope would deliver speeches. Dermot would discuss these Christmas messages with Patrick and Brendan, as he'd discussed them in the past with Mr Joyce. He would be as kind as ever. He would console Bridget and Cathal and Tom by saying that Mr Joyce hadn't been up to the journey. And whenever she looked at him she would remember the Christmases of the past. She would feel ashamed of him, and of herself.